Just Another Girl

A NOVEL

melody carlson

Revell

a division of Baker Publishing Group
Grand Rapids, Michigan

© 2009 by Melody Carlson

Published by Revell
a division of Baker Publishing Group
P.O. Box 6287, Grand Rapids, MI 49516-6287
www.revellbooks.com

Second printing, June 2009

Printed in the United States of America

All rights reserved. No part of this publication may be reproduced, stored in a retrieval system, or transmitted in any form or by any means—for example, electronic, photocopy, recording—without the prior written permission of the publisher. The only exception is brief quotations in printed reviews.

Library of Congress Cataloging-in-Publication Data
Carlson, Melody.
    Just another girl : a novel / Melody Carlson.
       p. cm.
    Summary: Sixteen-year-old Aster, caught between a self-absorbed older sister and a mentally-disabled younger one, yearns for a normal life and, with her first boyfriend's encouragement and trust in God, she begins to make things better.
    ISBN 978-0-8007-3257-8 (pbk.)
    [1. Middle-born children—Fiction. 2. Sisters—Fiction. 3. People with mental disabilities—Fiction. 4. Dating (Social customs)—Fiction. 5. Single-parent families—Fiction. 6. Family problems—Fiction. 7. Christian life—Fiction.] I. Title.
PZ7.C216637Jtt 2009
[Fic]—dc22
                                                  2008033779

This book is a work of fiction. Names, characters, places, and incidents are the product of the author's imagination or are used fictitiously. Any resemblance to actual events, locales, or persons, living or dead, is coincidental.

Prologue

For as long as I can remember, I've been stuck in the middle. Like being dealt a loser's hand with no more turns to take, my luck seemed to run out even before I was born. My older sister, Rose, got all the good stuff. Not only did she get the looks in the family, but being an energetic and fairly demanding child, she got the best part of my parents' attention too. I'm pretty sure this is true, because I've seen all the photos of young Rose with my parents—happy snapshots of the three of them laughing and having fun, all taken before I came along.

By the time I was born, only two years later, my mom was already getting a little worn-out by Rose's antics. And I've heard that my dad was severely disappointed that I was not the son he'd been longing for. If I'd been a boy, I would've been named Norman Nelson Flynn, after my dad, but because I was just another girl, my dad left the name-assigning task to my mother, a frustrated botanist who never graduated from college. Naturally, she decided to call me Aster. This is the name of a common and insignificant little flower that's not very pretty—some people even consider it a weed. Of course, my mom swears she loves asters for their simplicity and hardiness, but I'm still not convinced.

When I was about two, the third baby came along, and if it wasn't bad enough that she was *another* girl (my dad had already purchased an expensive baseball mitt for her), she also suffered from birth defects. Fortunately for this baby, she was quiet and good-natured, and so soft and creamy-white-looking that my mother named her Lily.

My dad hung around for a few more years, but it was easy to see, even for a little kid, that the man was miserable. I remember trying my best to make him happy. And knowing his aversion to his youngest daughter and her special needs, I would try to humor Lily if she ever cried when he was around. I would even try to act like a boy and play ball with Dad in the yard. But, looking back, I can see now that we were steadily losing him. And just before I turned ten, Dad left our house for work one day and never came back. That's when my mom gave me Lily. "You take care of her," she said that summer day. "She likes you."

That was seven years ago, and it seems like I've been taking care of Lily ever since. It's not that I don't love Lily. I do. But sometimes I just get tired, or, like my mom likes to say about herself, "I'm totally burned-out." Of course, I don't say this back to my mom because that would be like throwing fuel onto the fire. Why go there? But sometimes, and more often lately, I think that I deserve to have a life of my own too.

1

"I don't wanna wear dat!" Lily shouts as I hold out what used to be her favorite shirt. It's an oversized and faded pink T-shirt with what was once a smiling Minnie Mouse on the front. This T-shirt could give the impression that we've been to Disneyland, which is not true. Not even close to true.

"Come on, Lily," I urge. "We need to get ready to go."

"No!" She juts out her chin and attempts to fold her arms across her chest, but I notice her struggle to perform this old stubborn posture, since her chest, like the rest of her body, has been growing a lot this past year. Even though she's not quite fifteen, and I'm almost seventeen, the cup size on her bra is a double D while I'm barely an A. Not that I'm jealous exactly.

I pretend to study the pink T-shirt, seeing that Minnie's face is partially rubbed off, which makes the rodent look slightly disgruntled—sort of how I'm feeling at the moment. But I force a smile and say, "But, Lily, this is your *favorite* shirt."

"Not today!" she grunts back at me with a frown that creases her pale, freckled forehead. Lily's monotone voice has always been gravelly, fairly deep, and loud enough to irritate some people, like Rose in particular. But then Rose has no patience for anyone. I have noticed that Lily's voice has gotten even deeper and louder this summer. In fact, my little sister has changed in all sorts of ways. Besides the big breasts, she's gotten a lot heavier. She's not as tall as I am, but she outweighs me by nearly fifty pounds. That can be scary sometimes, especially when she decides she wants to be difficult or go her own way and things turn physical—which I try to avoid at all costs.

I hold up the T-shirt hopefully. It's the only clean thing in her drawer today. I don't want to dig through the dirty laundry, and there's no time to do a quick load. "But Minnie will be so sad if you leave her home, Lily. Don't you want to—"

"No!"

"Okay." I put on my cheerful voice since I do not need a full-blown confrontation right now. All I have to do is get Lily dressed and down to the recreation center, and I can be blissfully free of her until four o'clock this afternoon. I've already packed her lunch with her favorites (a peanut butter and strawberry jelly sandwich on white bread, a not too ripe and not too green banana, and a bag of plain but rippled potato chips), as well as her swim bag with her tangerine swimsuit and matching goggles. But if I don't get her there by ten, she will miss the activities bus, and I'll be stuck with her all day long. "What *do* you want to wear, Lily?"

She points to my T-shirt. "That."

I look down at my olive green Gap T-shirt. I saved up for this shirt, and it fits me perfectly. I do *not* want to loan it to Lily. "It's too small for you," I say quietly. I head for her closet to dig through her dirty laundry basket.

"No, it's not!" she shouts. "You're older than me, Aster. You're bigger than me."

I'm digging through the stinking laundry basket now, trying to find a shirt that somehow resembles my Gap shirt, something to smooth this thing over and get us out the door. Finally I find a bright green tank top and hold it up. It's totally wrinkled and smells like old sweat and peanut butter and who knows what else, but it'll have to do. "This is green like my shirt," I say in my happy voice. "And this color looks so good on you."

"No!"

"But if you wear this," I say in a tempting voice, lifting my brows in an appealing way, "we'll *both* have on green shirts. We'll be alike, Lily. Like sisters!"

Lily starts to smile now. "Like sistahs?"

I nod. "Yes. Both in green. And we both have greenish eyes too. Cool, huh? Like sisters."

She nods too. "Yeah, cool. Like sistahs."

I hear Rose make a loud snort of a laugh from the hallway, and I want to strangle her. "Yeah, right," she says. "You'll look just like twins!"

"Yes, we will," I say quickly. But it's too late. Lily may be mentally slow, but she is quick to feel Rose's jabs. She's had years of training, and Rose isn't exactly subtle.

"No, no, no!" Lily shouts, sitting back on her twin bed now. She's still wearing the threadbare top of her teddy-bear pajamas, and she folds her hands across her front as she rocks back and forth repeating, "Not like twins . . . not like twins . . . Aster not my twin! Rose, you know Aster not my twin!"

I step out into the hallway and glare at my older sister. "Thanks a lot!"

But she just laughs. "What's wrong? You don't want to be Lily's twin today?"

"All I want is to get her to the rec center on time," I snap. Rose doesn't even react as she checks out her flawless image in the bathroom mirror. She's been primping for at least an hour. "But maybe you'd like to take her instead."

"Sorry, Aster, but *I* have to go to work." She slips a gold hoop into her left ear. "I have a job."

"Yeah, right." I roll my eyes as I envision her so-called job. Rose "works" in a cheesy shop called Delilah's, where she pushes makeup, hair products, and overpriced accessories. It's in the air-conditioned mall, and she mostly just stands around or chats with her friends. She might sell a few trinkets or give some of her "beauty" advice. Or, if she's really paying attention, she occasionally spots a shoplifter in the act and calls for security, then comes home and brags about how important she is and how hard she works. Tough life.

"You're just jealous." She cocks her head ever so slightly,

tilting her chin up as if she's striking a pose for a camera. Rose thinks she has what it takes to model professionally. I have my doubts, but I keep them to myself.

I bite my lower lip and listen to Lily. She's still in her room, pouting and pounding on something, probably her Little Mermaid pillow, which has seen better days. She's also muttering to herself about how mean Rose and I are, how she's going to tell Mom all about it when she gets home from work, and how we'll both be sorry then. I glance at my watch and realize that Rose might be my only chance now. I force a smile. "Can you drop us off on your way to the mall, Rose?" I beg. "It's on the way."

"Only if you're ready to go *right now*." She fluffs her already perfect strawberry blonde bangs and smiles at her reflection one last time. "And I mean now—not two minutes from now."

"You know that's impossible, Rose."

She just shrugs. "Sorry, I can't be late to work."

"We would've been ready if you hadn't interfered."

But she doesn't care. She never has. All Rose thinks about is Rose.

I hurry back to Lily, trying the green T-shirt routine once again. I use every persuasive trick I know, but she is not buying it, and the clock is steadily ticking. I can almost see the glint in her eyes as she digs in her heels now. She relishes the fact that she is in total control of this situation, fully aware that she has the power to create chaos in my life whenever she chooses to take the difficult route. That's the road we're stuck on this morning.

"You won't get to see your friends today," I point out.

"I don't care."

"You won't get to go swimming at the big pool." The tone of my voice gets higher at the end of each sentence—my enticing pitch, laced with desperation.

"I don't care."

"You won't have your picnic lunch at the park."

But it's like talking to a stone—a stone that is now rocking back and forth and yelling, "I don't care," at regular intervals. I want to cover my ears and scream. I want to tell her to shut up, shut up, shut up! But I know that won't help. Besides, I know that her life isn't exactly easy. Unlike some of her challenged friends, Lily is not mentally impaired enough to be blissfully oblivious to the teasing that occurs regularly in her life. And yet she's not mentally capable of dealing with the cruelty either. Sometimes she even gets accepted as "normal," although that never lasts for long once they figure things out. It's like she's caught between two worlds. Or kind of like me—she's stuck in the middle.

It's five minutes until ten, and Rose is long gone. I know there's probably not enough time to walk Lily to the rec center now, even if we had one of our pretend races, where I always act tired and let Lily win, and she gives me a hard time for being "slow." But it gets us there sooner. Still, I know there's a slight possibility that other kids are acting out or someone forgot something or needs to use the bathroom. It's entirely possible and not unlikely that the bus might be getting a late start too. Call me a desperate optimist, but I'm not ready to give up my freedom for today. Not yet.

In fact, I'm so desperate that I actually consider loaning Lily my Gap T-shirt, even though it would be skintight and she'd probably look indecent, plus my shirt would be completely ruined. Sort of like my life.

2

Unwilling to give up and hoping I can find a shirt to tempt Lily, I dash back to my room—rather, the room I share with Rose, the room that Rose rules. She still resents that I insisted on switching from sharing a room with Lily. After more than ten years of listening to Lily belch, fart, throw tantrums, or wake up screaming from a nightmare, I told Mom that I either moved in with Rose or moved out. I was nearly thirteen at the time and felt the need for some autonomy (that means some control over my own life, although it's laughable). Anyway, Mom caved and Rose raged. In the end, I'm not even sure it was worth it. At least when I shared a room with Lily, I sort of ruled—or at least I told myself I did.

I rummage through my half of the closet (okay, *half* is a real stretch, it's actually more like a fourth) until I finally find a shirt that might work for Lily. It's a red and white soccer jersey that she used to lust after on a regular basis. But to seal the deal, I quickly pull off my Gap shirt and pull on the jersey.

"So, Lily," I say as I casually meander back into her messy

room. "I guess you just want to be stuck home all day. You can help me do the laundry, and then we'll clean the garage and work in—"

"No!" she says. "I don't wanna stay home."

"Well, do you want to wear your pajamas to the—"

"No!" She's staring at my jersey now. "Why you wearing dat, Aster?"

"Because I want to."

Her eyes narrow with suspicion. "You play soccer today?"

"No. I just felt like wearing it, Lily. It's comfortable." I kind of strut now, like I think I'm being really fashionable.

She stands up, and with her lower lip sticking out, she points at me. "I wanna wear dat shirt!"

And just like that, I rip off the shirt and toss it at her. "Fine," I say as if I'm miffed. "You want all my best things." Then I dash back to my room and pull my Gap shirt back on, and within seconds I have grabbed up her scruffy pink backpack and am running for the front door. "You probably even think you can run faster than me too."

"I can! I can!" she yells as she clumps through the house behind me.

"I'll beat you to the corner," I yell as I open the door. I wait for her to run past me and then lock it. I take off after her, playing the game, pretending like she's beating me and I can't stand it.

We're almost to the first corner when I see a shiny white Chevy pickup driving toward us, slowing down at the intersection as if to see what we're doing. I know Owen Swanson owns that pickup. Rather, his dad owns that pickup because his dad also owns Swanson Chevrolet, where Owen gets the use of vehicles fresh off the lot—maybe it's a form of advertising. Anyway, during the last week of school, Owen was driving around in that white pickup, showing off his latest set of wheels.

Why am I so cognizant of this fact? Because, like dozens of other girls, I've been watching Owen Swanson for years. Sure, he's totally out of my league, but that doesn't mean I can't look. I just wish that he wasn't looking my way right now. The last thing I want this morning is to be spotted by Owen—to be seen running down the street like a lunatic, pretending I can't even catch my mentally retarded sister, and struggling along like my legs are full of cement. And, oh crud, I'm still holding her stupid Hello Kitty backpack. I resist the urge to toss down the pack and run in the opposite direction.

"Where's the fire?" Owen calls out casually.

I look at him with wide eyes, shocked to see that he's actually talking to me. "Huh?" I shove the backpack toward Lily.

"Are you late for something?"

"We going to the rec center," Lily answers for me. She stands up proudly now, as if she thinks that Owen is directing his question to her. Is she actually sticking her chest out at him? Mom needs to talk to her again.

"Need a ride?" he offers.

I'm stunned now. Is he kidding?

"Not supposed to ride wif strangers," Lily chirps. She's still sticking her chest out and smiling smugly.

"I'm not a stranger," Owen says. "I know Aster."

I cannot believe he actually knows my name. Owen Swanson knows my name! "We're late," I say stupidly. Like, duh, hasn't that been established?

"Come on," he urges. "I'll take you there."

And the next thing I know, I'm shoving Lily and her pink backpack into the pickup, she's sitting between Owen and me, and he's driving us toward the rec center.

"We going swimming today," Lily tells him. "Then we eat lunch in the park."

"Nice." He says this almost like he means it, which I know is not possible. None of this seems possible, and I try not to lean over and stare at him. I feel like I'm having an out-of-body experience. Or maybe I just stepped into the Twilight Zone. But I cannot believe that Owen Swanson is driving me and my retarded sister around town in his brand-new truck.

"This is a nice pickup," I say, feeling like an idiot. Seriously, couldn't I think of something more intelligent to say?

"Thanks," he says. "I was thinking about switching back to a car, though. I have to pay for my own gas, and this isn't exactly economic—"

"The bus!" Lily cries, pointing to the bus already going down the street.

"Oh no." I watch as the bus turns directly onto the expressway. "We're too late."

"Is the bus going to the pool?" Owen asks.

"Stanley Pool," I say.

"The one with waves," Lily mutters. She sounds like she's about to cry. "Why didn't they wait for me, Aster?"

"I told you, Lily." I shake my finger at her to make a point. "You can't be late like that."

"I wanna go to the pool," she says, sobbing. "It's not fair!"

"I can drive you over there," Owen offers.

"Yes, yes!" Lily cries. "You can! You can drive me there."

"You don't mind?" I ask hopefully.

"No problem. I wasn't doing anything anyway." Owen looks slightly perplexed, like he's wondering how he got into this mess. But he turns toward the expressway, and it seems the decision has been made.

Lily claps her hands now, pointing to the big yellow bus now only a few cars ahead of us. "Catch them!" she cries.

"I'll do better than that." Owen steps on it and switches to the fast lane. "I'll pass them, and we'll beat them there."

"Yes!" Lily says, clapping her hands even more frantically. "We'll beat them!"

And we do beat them. In less than ten minutes we're there. "Here you go." Owen looks relieved as he pulls in front of the pool's entrance. "Enjoy your swim, ladies."

Lily laughs as she reaches for her Hello Kitty pack. "Aster's not going swimming," she says like it's a joke. "Just me, silly. Me and my friends in the bus. Then we go to the park to play."

"Oh?" Owen glances at me as I climb from the pickup and help Lily out. "So what are you going to do, Aster?"

I kind of shrug, wishing I'd thought to grab my purse and my bus pass. I can't imagine how boring it will be to be stuck here all day, although I do have my cell phone in my pocket, so I might be able to guilt Rose into giving me a ride home during her lunch break. Or not.

"Need a ride back?"

"Sort of."

"Hop in."

I glance over to where the bus is pulling up behind us to unload the other kids now. "Do you mind if I go tell the director that Lily's here first?"

"No problem."

Of course, Lily has already run ahead of me and is now informing her special friends about how she got to ride in that cool white truck and how we passed the bus and beat them . . . yada, yada, yada. I quickly find Kellie Martin, the woman in charge of the park district's special program, and I explain about Lily missing the bus.

"Well, I'm glad you made it," she says as Lily greets her with a big bear hug.

"Me too," Lily says.

"Have fun," I tell her.

"Bye, Aster." Lily waves, then puckers up her lips with an impish expression. "Don't you kiss that cute boy!"

Naturally she's said this loudly enough for everyone in the

parking lot and several blocks away to hear her. I make a face at her, and then, trying to appear nonchalant, I shove my hands into the pockets of my khaki shorts and stroll back to the pickup. Oh, Lily, whatever will we do with you?

"Everything okay?" Owen asks as I climb back in and fasten the seat belt.

"Yeah. I just needed to make sure they knew she was here."

"Do you always take care of her?" Owen asks as he pulls out of the parking lot.

"Not always." I consider this and wonder. "I mean, not 24-7. But I guess when it comes to getting Lily to where she needs to go and all that . . . yeah, that's kind of my responsibility."

"That's a big responsibility."

"Well, my mom works full-time. And she expects me to do what I can."

"And your parents are divorced, right?"

I glance at him, surprised that he knows this much about me. "Yeah . . . my dad left about seven years ago."

"I remember."

"You remember?"

"Sure. We were in fifth grade together. Remember, Mrs. Blanton's class?"

"You remember me from way back then?"

He laughs. "Sure. I thought you were cute with your red pigtails and freckles. And you were a killer soccer player."

I blink and feel tempted to pinch myself. "Yeah, right."

"You were."

I want to ask if that means he thought I was cute or a killer soccer player, but I don't. Both are pretty high compliments. And so I just sit there in shock, trying to wrap my head around this whole thing. How is it possible that Owen Swanson is not only chauffeuring me around town, but that he thought I was cute back in fifth grade? Then I remember how Owen used to be friendly to me when we were kids. He was just an all-around nice guy back then. But when we all moved to middle school, everything seemed to change. Owen grew a few inches, got rid of his braces, and got better at sports. As a result he became extremely popular.

It all seemed to happen so quickly. About that same time, I lost my old best friend, the only real best friend I'd ever had. Or so I thought at the time. Katie Wick and I had been inseparable up until middle school. But Katie, like Owen, got popular. In fact, I think they even went together for a while. Not that I was privy to these things—well, other than observation. I did not get swooped up into that popular clique, and consequently Katie's and my paths parted. That's when I started to live up to my name (asters are shy and easily overshadowed by other more flamboyant blooms) and turned into a real wallflower.

I suppose it didn't help matters that my mom suddenly decided that since I was almost twelve and "practically an adult," I should assume even more of the responsibility of caring for Lily. This meant getting her to and from her special class in school as well as other activities, and so I could be seen drag-

21

ging her around town, placating her when she had a tantrum, defending her if someone teased . . . whatever it took.

"It's funny," Owen says as he exits the expressway, "but you kind of seemed to disappear off the radar after grade school. Did you move away for a while or something?"

I sort of laugh. "No, we never moved. You just got too popular to notice someone like me."

He rolls his eyes and shakes his head. "Yeah, whatever."

"Seriously," I persist, thinking I've got nothing to lose. "You were Mr. Popularity, and I was Miss Nobody. It's no surprise that you didn't know I was still around. And I guess I kept a low profile too."

He clears his throat. "And, well, there was that thing with your sister."

I nod. "Oh yeah, let's not forget I was that pathetic loser dragging around her retard sister—"

"I didn't say that!"

"I know . . . at least you didn't today. But you might have back then. I mean, pretty much everyone else did in middle school. But that was a long time ago." I'd like to act like it's all behind me now. Like high school kids are more mature . . . and for the most part they are. But there are still some idiots out there.

I'm about to tell him to turn on Larch Street, but he seems to know the way to my house. Once again, I'm surprised.

"I don't know why kids are so mean," he says as he pulls into my driveway.

"Because they're ignorant," I suggest.

"Fortunately, we grow up eventually, and hopefully, we get less ignorant."

"Thanks for the ride," I say as I reach for the door handle.

"No problem."

"Seriously, I really appreciate it. If you hadn't got Lily to the pool, I would've been stuck with her all day." I sigh. "I mean, I do love my sister, but sometimes I need a break."

"So what are you going to do with your break?"

I consider admitting that I'm going to do about three loads of laundry and clean the kitchen and do a few other boring chores, but I realize how pitiful that sounds. I mean, get real, he's going to think I've got a serious Cinderella complex. And I don't. I mean, I do have a life. Don't I?

"Oh, I don't know," I say as I slowly open the door. "It's such a pretty day . . . maybe I'll take a bike ride."

"Want any company?" he says quickly.

"Seriously?"

"Yeah. I haven't ridden my bike in ages. It sounds kind of fun."

"Seriously?" I say again, knowing how idiotic I must sound. I actually do have a vocabulary, why don't I use it?

"Yeah. I used to ride the river trail all the time before I started driving. Then bike riding just seemed, well, you know . . . kinda uncool."

"But it's not kinda uncool now?"

He shrugs. "I'm not so sure I care about all that anymore."

Okay, I'm trying not to look overly stunned. I mean, people change, right? Maybe Owen Swanson is changing too. After all, we're going to be seniors in the fall . . . maybe it is about time to grow up.

"So, how about it?"

"I guess that'd be okay," I say.

"I'll need to go home and get my bike." He frowns. "I probably need to check the tires and mechanical stuff since it's been sitting around for a couple of years. Do you mind waiting?"

"That's fine," I say, realizing this will buy me some time to put in a load of laundry and maybe even clean up the kitchen.

"How about I come back here around noon then?"

"Sure, that sounds good." Now I actually smile at him, not too big though. I don't want to seem overly eager. But he smiles back at me with those straight white teeth and sparkling blue eyes, and suddenly I'm thinking that the oxygen supply to my brain has just been cut off. But I keep it chill and just wave, then turn and jog up to the front door. I don't even look back as I unlock the door.

My hands are actually shaking when I let myself in. Then I lean back against the closed door. I take in a slow, deep breath and wonder if I just imagined the whole thing. No way would Owen Swanson invite himself to go on a bike ride with me today—that is totally surreal. Maybe it was just my imagination messing with me. Just wishful thinking. A crazy daydream.

Even so, I decide to be ready. Just in case it's for real.

3

Since losing Katie to popularity, I've never had another real honest-to-goodness best friend. Not like the other girls that I see paired up around school and at malls and everywhere, acting like they're part of some secret society where I'll never belong. But Crystal is the closest thing to a best friend. And to be fair, she might even assume that I'm her best friend since she probably spends more time with me than anyone else, and that's not saying much. Oh, she picks Lily and me up to go to youth group, and sometimes we go to the mall together, but it's not like we're close. Not really. I happen to know that Lily makes Crystal uncomfortable. And if she calls and invites me to do something, then discovers that Lily will have to come, she sometimes changes her mind. And we don't go. Naturally, I don't question this. Why should I? It's not like we're real best friends.

Even so, I suddenly have this inexplicable urge to call up my "best friend" and tell her that Owen Swanson and I are going on a bike ride together and that I cannot believe it and that is it possible he likes me? But I control myself. For one thing, I'm still not convinced that I'm not hallucinating. For another thing, he could just be playing a mean joke on me. And, finally, although I like Crystal just fine—I mean, she's great for a "casual" friend—I'm just not ready to divulge anything too personal to her. As corny as it sounds, I'm not ready for that kind of commitment.

I put myself into fast speed and throw in a load of laundry, sort out the next two, and line up the baskets so they'll be ready to go. Then I dash into the kitchen, and in record time I have the dishwasher loaded and running and the counters wiped. The sink and stove will have to wait. Then I swoop through the living room (my mother's personal pet peeve is seeing the living room trashed) and grab up miscellaneous items strewn about—mostly from Lily. And, with a full load of Lily's junk, I heave it into her room, which smells like someone put a dead fish under her bed, but I'm guessing it's her tennis shoes. I close the door and decide to deal with that later.

I do a quick cleanup in the bathroom. It's so cluttered with Rose's jewelry and makeup and hair stuff that it's nearly impossible to do a thorough job. In fact, it's no wonder her paychecks are so minimal, since I'm sure she must waste half of her earnings on this junk. Still, if I touch or move any of her things, she throws a huge hissy fit. Even Lily is afraid to touch Rose's belongings, although she does occasionally—and even more since she's getting older. Lily thinks that she should be able to wear makeup and jewelry like Rose, but Mom keeps putting her foot down, which I think is a little unfair since both Rose and I were allowed to do pretty much what we wanted to when we were Lily's age. "But Lily is special," Mom points out. "We don't want her to grow up too fast."

Of course, I wonder what that's supposed to mean since, duh, it's not like she's ever going to grow up anyway. Her mental capacity is supposedly equivalent to a five-year-old. She recognizes some letters and numbers and can write her name and a few other short words like "no" and "bye" and "Mom." But that's about it.

Still, what would it hurt if she was allowed a little lip gloss and blush if she wants it? And yet this is a battle I'm not willing to fight. If Mom wants to keep Lily as her little girl forever, that's her choice. The problem is that Mom doesn't seem to notice that, despite Lily's stunted mental capacity, her body is growing up. But there's a lot that Mom doesn't seem to notice.

Anyway, I don't want to think about that now. I don't want to think about Lily or Rose or Mom. I want to be selfish and think only about me, me, me.

I stare at my image in the bathroom mirror, wondering what I might possibly do to enhance my appearance. Okay, that probably seems stupid in light of the fact that I caught Owen's eye without enhancing a single thing. Still . . . I can't help that I care, can I? I mean, I'm a girl. I'm almost seventeen. One of the coolest guys seems to be looking my way. And I know what my competition looks like. Not that I can compete. I'm pretty sure I can't. But I can't just give in either.

I realize there's not much that can be done with my hair on such short notice. Rose has suggested numerous times that I should get it highlighted and cut into layers to calm down the thickness and natural waves, but I'm not sure that would really be an improvement. Plus I'd have to fuss with it and style it—and in my opinion, that's a waste of time, energy, and money. One time I tallied up all the time that Rose spends on her hair, and it was more than five hundred hours a year. I have no idea how much she spends on hair products and salon visits.

My hair, which most people call red, I call auburn. I like to imagine that it's the color of mahogany. It's not really that dark, but I hope it will be someday. And today it's pulled back in a messy ponytail that goes midway to my back. I take it down and spend about five minutes attempting to tame my mane, which is not happening. In fact, it's actually getting worse. Finally I give up completely and simply put it back in the ponytail, which I realize looked better before I messed with it. In fact, that's just what it needs—to be messy again. So I take my hair down and shake it around and mess it up, then I quickly put the ponytail back in. Better.

Next I examine my face. Fortunately, my freckles have faded a bit. When I was little, kids used to accuse me of having the measles. Now my freckles sort of blend together and almost look like a tan. But my lips, as usual, are too pale. It's the curse of redheads to have overly pale lips. So I decide to "borrow" some of Rose's latest beauty discovery—a gloss that's supposed to plump your lips. I apply a generous coat of peony and watch to see if my lips get bigger. Actually, I don't think they need to be any bigger, but it's fun to see if anything happens. The lip gloss actually tingles a bit, but the color is kind of nice. Then I carefully put the tube of gloss back exactly where I got it.

Now I look at my eyes. My mom says they're just like my dad's. Of course, when she says this she's usually frowning, and I know she doesn't mean it as a compliment. What she's really saying is, "You remind me of your father, and he's not someone I want to be reminded of, so why don't you make yourself scarce?" And that's what I usually do.

Anyway, my eyes are hazel, which to me looks like a mix of muddy colors. Like when I'm painting with watercolors and am too impatient to wait for the paint to dry before I apply another color, so the painting becomes muddy and ruined. Or like God couldn't decide, so he threw in some leftover green and brown and blue and even some flecks of gold. Rose, who has beautiful blue eyes, told me that I should get tinted contacts. "Green," she recommended after studying me carefully. "That would be the right color for you." But the thought of putting something in my eye is too freaky.

Still, I decide that some brown mascara on my pale lashes (another curse of the redhead) won't hurt. But after that, I don't really see what else I can do in the makeup department without ending up looking like a clown. I've been down that road before, and today, if Owen does show up, I do not want to go down it again. I still remember the time when Rose "fixed me up" for the homecoming dance when I was a sophomore. Crystal and I had decided to go, and Rose, who was a senior then, insisted we should "dress up." So we did.

Rose, who had just started working at Delilah's, used this opportunity to turn us into her personal guinea pigs. Of course, I didn't realize this at the time. I actually thought it was sweet that she was giving us so much time and attention. And, being fifteen and not too experienced in the world of makeup and fashion, I let Rose do her thing. So did Crystal. Like guinea pigs being led to the slaughter, we stupidly let her turn us into clowns. Then she drove us to the dance—a dance she was "too mature" to go to herself. But when we got inside, we knew it was a mistake. No one else was dressed up like we were. And no one had makeup that looked anything like ours. I'm sure Rose laughed all the way home. I'm also sure that we would've been a hit on the rundown section of Main Street, but at Jackson High, we were losers.

"Don't think about things like that!" I say sharply to myself. "Owen might be here in less than twenty minutes." I only talk to myself like this when I'm feeling desperate and when I know I'm home alone. I make a quick run to the laundry room and put the wet clothes in the dryer, then start the next load in the washer. Not bad. I'm also done with my chores, and it's not even noon yet. Maybe I should do housework on fast speed all the time.

I run back to the hallway mirror and look at my whole reflection, wondering if I should change my clothes. But wouldn't that look weird? Or like I was trying too hard? Besides, this Gap T-shirt looks good on me. And what's better than these khaki shorts for riding a bike? Of course, the flip-flops won't do. Flip-flops on a bike is like a wreck waiting to happen.

I stand there just looking at myself now. I grew nearly three inches this past year. My mom thought I already had my height—a neat five foot seven just like her. And then, wham, I sprouted to almost five foot ten in just a few months. "It's all in your legs," Mom pointed out. "You could probably get a job modeling at O'Leary's with those legs, Aster." Of course, this had aggravated Rose to no end. She's the one who wants to be a professional model, but she's only five foot six.

Not that she or anyone else particularly cares to model at O'Leary's. That's the clothing store that our mother has managed for as long as I can remember. We call it "the old lady store" because of the kind of stuff they carry. They have seasonal fashion shows that all the old ladies in town faithfully attend. Thankfully, I've never had to model for any of them. They mostly use mature women to show off their fine threads.

I'm still standing in front of the hallway mirror daydreaming when I hear the doorbell ring. Hoping that it's Owen, I kick off my flip-flops, grab a pair of white (or once-white) Adidas shoes, and race for the front door. But then I wonder what I should do—invite him in? Ugh, I don't want him to see our old, worn furniture. But then I realize, what difference does it make? I mean, it's not like I can pretend I'm something I'm not.

"Hey," I say calmly as I open the door. "You're early."

"Yeah." He nods back to where his bike is parked on the sidewalk in front of his pickup. "The old bike was in better shape than I expected."

"It's a mountain bike," I say, as if he doesn't already know this.

"Yeah, but it's okay for streets too." He looks slightly embarrassed. "I mean, it's not that fast, but I used to like to ride trails and—"

"Mine is a mountain bike too," I say quickly. "I used to ride trails too."

"Cool." He looks relieved.

I'm biting my lower lip now, still caught in the shall-I-invite-him-in-or-not dilemma. "How about if I meet you in front," I say. "My bike's still in the garage."

"Great."

So I lock the front door and hurry out to the garage, but then I realize I'll have to open the garage door and reveal the disaster that's in there. Still, there is no getting the bike out without doing that. Too bad I didn't consider it earlier. I could've had my bike out front and ready to roll.

I run back inside and into the garage, holding my breath as I push the garage door opener. I watch as the old door slowly rattles and cranks up, like it too knows that embarrassment is in store.

"This garage is a total mess," I announce to Owen as I roll out my bike and park it in the driveway. Like he can't see that for himself. Not to mention it smells horrid in there. I wonder if there's a dead animal tucked in a corner somewhere.

I see him staring back into the dim shadows of scary-looking boxes and plastic bags and all kinds of junk that everyone in my household seems to think is acceptable to toss back here and forget. "I'm supposed to clean it out this summer, but I just haven't gotten to it yet." I kind of laugh as I go back to close the door. "It's not like I'm looking forward to it."

"It must be rough not having a dad around," he says as I push the automatic button, then leap out over the infrared beam.

I can hear the door groan noisily behind me, slowly grinding its way back down. "Yeah, sometimes."

"Do you see your dad much?"

"Not much." Then I notice that Owen's bike helmet is strapped over his seat. "Are you wearing that?" I ask. I realize that mine is probably buried somewhere deep in that awful garage.

He shrugs. "Not necessarily. It was just there." He laughs. "The last time I rode I was probably under sixteen and didn't want to get a ticket."

"Interesting that they think we should be safer on our bikes before we turn sixteen. I mean, do they see how some kids drive?"

"I'm a good driver," he says as he tosses his helmet into the back of his pickup.

"Yeah, but do you remember how to ride a bike?" I swing a

leg over, hop onto the seat, and take off. I can hear him yelling behind me, telling me to slow down, to wait up, but I'm so outta there. It's like I want to escape. Not from him exactly, but maybe just from my life. Besides, I want to see what this boy's made of!

4

"You didn't warn me it was going to be a race," Owen huffs when he finally catches me at the foot of the trail in River Park.

"Sorry." I grin sheepishly. "I just got caught up in the moment."

"You're a good rider."

"Thanks. Did I wear you out?"

"Are you kidding? I was just getting warmed up."

His face is slightly flushed, and I'm curious as to what kind of shape this guy is actually in. He used to play most of the sports, but I haven't been paying that close of attention lately.

"Did you do track this year?"

He kind of laughs. "Is that some kind of insinuation? Like you think I'm not in my best form?"

I sort of shrug. "No . . . just curious."

"As a matter of fact, I didn't do track. Did you?"

"As a matter of fact, I did." I don't admit that the only reason I did track was to get a break from Lily. As usual, I encouraged her to sign up to train for the Special Olympics, and when she balked, I told her I'd be doing track too. That cinched the deal, and the track coach seemed glad to have me back for another year, plus my high jump had improved thanks to my height. Even so, I do not plan to go out for track during my senior year, although Lily could change that too.

"So do you plan to go full-out on the trail too?" Owen says with a slightly concerned look.

"I don't know . . ." I narrow my eyes as if I'm sizing him up. "I could take it easy on you. By the way, why didn't you go out for track? You used to be the best hurdler out there."

"I did something to my knee at the end of basketball season." He bends down to rub his right knee, which I now notice has two very small scars on either side. "I had surgery in March, and I wasn't supposed to do anything for six weeks. Kind of wiped out track season for me."

"Sorry," I say, feeling guilty now. "If I'd known, I would've slowed down."

He laughs. "Actually, bike riding is one of the things that the doctor did recommend. That and swimming and some other boring exercises. But I'm pretty much good to go now, just a little out of shape . . . as you probably noticed."

Now I feel really bad. The poor guy's practically a cripple, and I'm out here running him into the ground. "I'll take it easier on the trail, okay?"

"Don't slow down for my sake." He's getting back into the saddle again, and I can tell by the glint in his eyes that he's about to take off, probably hoping to leave me in the dust. "This is just the kind of workout I've been needing," he calls as he takes off. Suddenly I'm eating his dust and wondering why it's always harder to keep up when you're the one who's behind. I'm sure it must be psychological.

But I have to admit it's kind of fun trailing Owen now. I can study his physique without him being aware. His broad shoulders are hunkered down slightly, his tan, muscular calves pump up and down, his narrow hips and waist . . . Okay, time to focus on my own form before I have a wreck. Then I wonder if that's not exactly what Owen was doing while riding behind me. Hopefully, he liked what he saw.

Suddenly I want to pinch myself. Is this for real? Am I really out here on a hot June day riding bikes with Owen Swanson? Seriously, it's almost like a date. Not that I'd know since I've never even been on a real date before. Oh, sure, a couple of guys have asked me out. One was a nerdish academic named Neal. We had geometry together, and sometimes he helped me. And, sure, he was nice enough, but not the kind of guy I could get excited about dating, plus he had this really bad case of acne. I'm not a snob, but I just have a hard time looking at the kind of zits that threaten to erupt at any given moment. Call me squeamish, but I know my limitations.

The other guy was just a hormonal jerk who seemed to have only one thing on his mind—as in S-E-X. I'm not kidding. Whenever he looks at me or any other female, including Mrs. Fowler, an English teacher who has to be in her fifties, it's like he's seeing us all naked. Really creepy. No girl in her right mind would go out with a perv like that!

But why am I thinking about guys like that when I'm out here riding bikes with Owen Swanson—Mr. McSteamy!

● ● ●

Finally we've ridden all the way to the mall park, and we're both pretty winded. "That was great," he says as we walk our bikes over to the picnic table area. "Just what I needed. I hope I didn't wear you out, Aster. Was I going too fast?"

"Not at all. I was letting you set the pace. But maybe we should call a taxi or something. I mean, will you be able to make it back okay?" I tease.

"Very funny."

"The truth is, I was having a hard time staying with you," I say. "You seem to have warmed up just fine."

"Except that I'm starving now—and thirsty. Want to grab a bite to eat before we head back?"

I shove my hand into an empty pocket and grimace. "Shoot, I didn't think to grab any—"

"Hey, this is my treat, Aster."

I shrug, trying to act like no big deal, like the word "date" isn't rumbling around in my head. "Cool."

So we park and lock our bikes, then head into the mall, which is about thirty degrees cooler than outside and rather shocking. Of course, the only thing I can think about as we walk toward the food court is that it's probably Rose's lunch break about now, and the last thing I want to do is run into her. I'm sure she'll say something totally embarrassing, plus she'll be sure to tell Mom and Lily about how she saw me out with a *guy*. And then the homeland inquisition will begin.

I'd really like to keep this thing—this whatever it is—with Owen to myself. I so don't want to see Rose. And I don't usually bother God with trivial requests like this since I know he has more important matters to tend to like wars and global warming, but I'm desperate. *Please, please, please . . . don't let me be seen by my older sister while we're—*

"Aster!"

I stop walking and take in a quick breath as I realize my silly prayer is too late. I've been spotted by my sister. "Hey, Rose," I say calmly, like it's nothing unusual for me to be strolling through the mall with the handsome and popular and so-out-of-my-league Owen Swanson.

"What's up?" she asks as she does a quick inventory of Owen. She has some kind of lime smoothie drink that she seems to have coordinated with her T-shirt. Does she do that on purpose?

"Not much," I say casually. "Uh, do you know Owen Swanson?" I give Owen a stiff smile. "This is my older sister, Rose."

He smiles politely and actually shakes her hand. His dad, the car salesman, must've trained him well. "Pleasure to meet you, Rose. I think I remember you from a couple years back. Aren't you my brother's age?"

"Wayne Swanson?" she says with a bright smile. "Yes, we

graduated together just over a year ago. Seems like longer than that now. So how is old Wayne doing anyway?"

"He just got home from his first year of college, and Dad's got him working at the lot for the whole summer." Owen chuckles. "I think it's to make up for some of Wayne's less-than-impressive grades this past year. He insisted on going to this hoity-toity private college, and the tuition was a little steep, and now our dad's a little miffed. Looks like old Wayne'll be hanging at Lincoln Community College next year."

"I've taken some classes there." Now Rose gets her superior expression, her chin out and her nose tilted up ever so slightly. "I suppose it's a little better than high school, but trust me, they don't call LCC *Last Chance College* for nothing." Then she makes an L shape with her thumb and forefinger, but thankfully, she doesn't thump her forehead with it. Talk about sophisticated.

But Owen just laughs, and I suppress the urge to point out that Rose may have *started* a couple of classes at that loser school, but she never finished them. Seriously, LCC might be the last chance for my big sister. It only adds to my aggravation to remember that she wasted precious tuition money that she somehow pressured our dad into paying for. Not that it's likely to happen again anytime soon.

"Well, you kids have fun." Rose tosses me a sly little look, which I pretend to ignore. "Nice meeting you, Owen. Tell your big brother hey for me."

"Sure will, Rose. Nice to meet you too."

I blow out a loud breath as we walk away. "Sorry about that."

"Huh?"

"Oh, Rose, she's kind of weird." I turn and look at him help-lessly. "In fact, my whole family is pretty weird."

He just smiles. "Aren't all families?"

Now I actually consider this. The truth is, I don't know for sure. I've always been pretty certain that my family was one of the strangest ones on the planet. But perhaps I'm wrong. Still, I'm relatively certain that Owen's family, despite his older brother's unfortunate grades, can't be nearly as peculiar as mine.

We cruise around the food court restaurants until we dis-cover that we both love gyros, which somehow seems like fate to me. I mean, how many seventeen-year-old guys would pick gyros on pita bread over a Big Mac or a Whopper? Is that merely a coincidence? I do not think so! Of course, he teases me when I order root beer to go with it. Well, I suppose we don't have to agree on everything.

"You know what I want to say?" he says as we sit down at one of the less messy tables. I do my best to wipe it down with napkins, but it's still sticky.

"What?"

"It's going to sound corny."

Okay, now I'm really interested. "What?" I demand.

"I seriously want to say, 'Aster Flynn, where have you been all my life?'"

Now I cannot help but laugh. But it's a horrible-sounding snort of a laugh. I think it's because I'm so excited that I'm practically giddy. I can't believe he just said that. But suddenly I get totally paranoid. I glance around with suspicion.

"What's wrong?"

"Okay, where are the cameras?" I demand.

"Huh?"

"Are you punking me?"

"What?"

"Where's Jamie Kennedy?"

"Is that show even still on?"

"I don't know." I look all around the semicrowded food court, but nothing seems out of line. No lights, no cameras. Not even a cell phone pointed in my direction. "But *are* you punking me?"

"No, of course not."

"Oh." Now I feel really stupid.

"Sorry." He looks slightly offended as he picks up his gyro and attempts a bite with the meat falling out from both ends and yogurt dripping.

"Were you serious?" I ask quietly. "I mean, what you just said a little bit ago?"

"I know, it sounded pretty lame."

"Well . . . unexpected anyway." I peel the wrapper off my straw and stick it in my root beer. I wonder, why does everyone think it's so cool to date anyway? Not that this is a date. I know that it's not. But, really, this isn't *that* fun. I mean, it's

42

kind of exciting and interesting. But it's also really stressful and nerve-racking, like I wouldn't be surprised if I broke out in hives. And what did he just say to me exactly? "Where have you been all my life?" Give me a break! He has got to be punking me. Either that or I'm asleep and dreaming this whole thing.

"It's just that you're pretty cool, Aster." He looks directly at me now. "And you're really pretty too. I don't know why I didn't notice you before."

This causes me to nearly choke on my first sip of root beer. Be still, my heart. Just breathe . . . and swallow. "Seriously?" I stare at him. "You think that *I* am cool?" Okay, I'm probably more blown away by the "pretty" comment. But I settle on "cool."

"I do."

"Well then . . ." I take another slow, cautious sip, careful not to choke, and I attempt to process this. Owen Swanson thinks that I, Aster Flynn, am cool—cool and pretty. That's a lot to absorb straight out of the blue. How does a girl respond to something like that? What do I say to him?

And suddenly my cell phone is ringing. That can only mean one thing. Trouble. The only one who ever calls me on my cell phone is Lily. It's basically her 9-1-1 number and the only reason Mom got me this phone.

"Sorry," I tell Owen. "I have to get this." I check the caller ID, and it is indeed my younger sister. "Hi, Lily," I say as lightly as I can. "What's up?"

She is sobbing. "As–As–Aster!"

"What? What is wrong?"

"I–I–I need you. Now!"

"Lily," I say in my calming voice. "Tell me what's wrong. Are you okay?"

"No!"

"Lily, you need to explain."

"I need you!" More sobbing.

"Lily?"

"Come and get me. Please! I'm–I'm bleeding . . . you know . . . the woman thing between the legs. I *need* you to bring those pad things! *Hurry!*"

Now I feel like the blood is draining from me as I close my phone and look at Owen. "It's Lily . . . there's a problem."

"Is she hurt?"

"Sort of," I admit. "I mean, she's, uh, bleeding."

"Oh, man, should we call for a paramedic or something?"

"No. It's that other kind of bleeding." I can feel the blood returning to my face now—throbbing in full force and probably making my cheeks bright red. "I need to take her some, uh, feminine hygiene products." Oh crud, did I just say that? Out loud?

His eyes get wide now, and I can tell this is way too much for him. Well, hey, it's way too much for me too. But it's my life. My sucky, crappy, messed-up, freaking life.

5

I take it back. I *do* have a Cinderella complex. And I am furious at my life—rather, my lack of a life. As I drive Rose's Toyota over to the park to pick up Lily, I'm feeling enraged over just about everything. I'm angry about my family, my MIA father, my checked-out mother, my demanding sisters, and even the slow car ahead of me. And I can't believe that I actually had to beg Rose to lend me her car. I threatened to call Mom and explain the whole situation. Then I reminded Rose that Mom still pays her insurance and that Rose is just as much Lily's sister as I am.

"Fine, but you better drive carefully," she warned me as she handed over her precious car keys on that silly pink rhinestone key chain. Then, more discreetly, she slipped a bulky sanitary pad to me, and I tucked it into a side pocket. "It's not a very good brand," she told me. "I swiped it from the employee bathroom."

"Thanks, I guess."

She leaned back against the counter. "So, where's McDreamy?"

"Owen?" I said his name absently, acting like I barely knew him, which I suppose is true.

"Yeah? Where'd he go?"

"Probably home," I said casually. I'd actually encouraged him to take off. He halfheartedly offered to go with me, to get his pickup and take me to the pool again, but I could tell he was pretty uncomfortable. I'm sure the idea of helping me rescue my messed-up retarded sister was overwhelming to a guy like him. I know that's a mean description of Lily, but it's just the way I'm feeling right now. And I suspect that Owen realized he was in over his head too. Anyway, he seemed relieved to make his getaway.

"Well, don't let Lily get blood on my new seat covers," Rose said as I was leaving the shop. Naturally several heads turned at that, although I'm sure Rose will straighten them out. She'll probably make up a story about how our sister was in an accident and how Rose sacrificially offered her car to rescue her. Rose always tries to come out smelling like a rose.

It's not until I'm halfway across town that I realize I don't even have my driver's license with me. So I'm very, very careful. But I'm still fuming. And I'm wondering why Kellie couldn't have dealt with this little fiasco at the park. But then I realize she probably has her hands full with all those other kids. To be honest, I don't know how she does it. And I can say this from experience, because she's talked me into assisting on these field trips before. It's no walk in the park.

To be fair, once Lily loses it, well, it's hard for anyone to deal with her. Anyone but me, I guess. My mom thinks I have the "magic touch" when it comes to Lily. But I think it's only because she put a spell on me so that I would be enslaved to Lily forever. See, there I go again, sounding like poor Cinderella.

I park Rose's car apart from any other vehicles so that I don't incur any door dings. (I know Rose will check.) Then I find Lily sitting on a cement bench a short distance from where her friends are playing. Her hair is still wet from the pool, and she's clutching her Hello Kitty backpack in front of her and scowling. And it just figures, she wore her white shorts today. I'd totally forgotten about that. Poor Lily.

"Come on, sis," I say.

"No." She firmly shakes her head from side to side, still clinging to her backpack like it's a life preserver.

"No?" I put my hands on my hips and wait.

"No."

"What? Are you going to sit there all day and all night? Like forever?"

"I can't stand up, *Aster*." You can tell Lily is mad when she really accentuates your name—it hisses out of her mouth like a curse.

"Are your legs broken?"

Her heavy brows pull together to give me her darkest, meanest look now. "My. Pants. *Aster*."

"Oh, right." I nod to Lily, then wave over to where Kellie is watching us from the play area. "You don't want your friends to see the blood on your shorts."

"Yeah."

So I reach for her pack, which she does not release. But even so I'm able to unzip it and dig out her damp Little Mermaid beach towel. I shake it open, then go behind the bench. "Stand up," I say. "No one can see you now. And we'll make your towel into a skirt for you."

"Okay." She sounds eager as she stands. I do my fashion magic, then walk around to see my "little" sister smiling with relief when she sees that I have managed to conceal the seat of her shorts, which really looked frightening. She must've gone for a while before she realized what was happening. I'm sure this must've been noticed by her friends—many who are too young to even understand why she'd have blood on her shorts. Maybe they were alarmed and thought she'd been hurt. I'm not sure I want to know.

"Now, you need to remember this little trick," I say as I walk her to the nearby bathroom. "You can always use a jacket or a sweater tied around your waist and hanging down to cover it up. I mean, if this ever happens again."

"Not ever again!" she sputters as I push the heavy door open.

"Well, hopefully not, Lily, but you never know. It's happened to me before."

"To you?" She looks at me with interest as I hold the stall door open for her. I take her backpack and hand her the slightly rumpled sanitary pad. Okay, perhaps it's a little late, but it can't hurt. As she goes into the stall, I feel guilty. Maybe this

48

is my fault. Maybe I need to keep track of Lily's cycle and make sure she has spare pads in her backpack.

"Yeah, Lily, it happens to everyone."

"Everyone?"

"Well, not guys. Remember this is just a girl thing. And it's no big deal, really. You just need to learn how to cover things up. And we'll keep extra pads in your backpack, just in case. We'll use that zipper pocket inside."

"Yes! Yes!"

It takes some coaching and time for her to get the pad in place. But I've taught her how to do this, and I know she can. Then she comes out, and I help her to rewrap her mermaid "skirt" around her thick middle, tucking the ends of the towel into the front of her shorts to hold it in place.

"Very nice," I say as we go back outside. "Now do you want to stay and play with your friends?"

"No!"

I figure as much. "Then let's go home." I hand her back her pack, and we head for the parking lot. It's even hotter now. I think it'll hit the mid-nineties before the day is over.

"Is Rose here?" Lily stops and points at Rose's car with a worried expression. Her fear is totally justified, because if Rose were here, she would probably scold and humiliate Lily for making such a mess of things.

"No, Rose is at work. She just let me use her car." I unlock the door and stare at Rose's new seat covers. They're some kind of Hawaiian print, hot pink and white, and in my opinion rather cheesy. Still, I know she'll kill me if Lily gets them bloody. "Wait," I say to Lily. "We need to put something down for you to sit on." I dig through the clutter of Rose's backseat until I find an old plastic shopping bag, which I transform into a seat cover. "There you go, sit on that."

Lily hums happily as I drive toward home. As always, she's oblivious as to how she just blew up my life. She probably doesn't even remember that "cute boy" who gave us a ride this morning. That's over and done. And Lily's life is always about Lily. Everything else is secondary.

But, to be fair, isn't everyone like that? Self-centered, self-absorbed, selfish? Except that most of us learn to conceal these unbecoming traits as we mature. Oh, they're still there, but we camouflage them so as not to offend. But people like Lily just let it all hang out. In a way that might be a good thing. It is what it is. What you see is what you get. No surprises. No tricks.

I let Lily into the house and, once again, show her the cupboard where the feminine hygiene products are kept. Then I go to the laundry room and rotate more loads of laundry from washer to dryer to basket before I return to check on Lily, who is now sitting on the edge of the bathtub and staring at one of Rose's fashion magazines.

"Hey, Lil," I say, holding up the basket of laundry. "After you get showered and cleaned up, do you want to fold these towels for me?"

"Okay." She grins like I've just invited her to eat cookie dough.

"Thanks! I'll put them on the couch." Sure, I know the towels won't be folded the way Mom likes, but I don't really care today. Maybe I'm starting to go through a rebellion or something. *But I just don't care.* Then I go to my room for my bag and my driver's license, only to remember I'll be riding my bike home. Toting a fashionable purse (okay, it's only an Isaac Mizrahi from Target) while riding a mountain bike? I don't think so. So I pocket my wallet and leave the faux leather bag behind.

"Where you going?" Lily asks, suddenly suspicious of the car keys in my hand. She does not like being left home alone— ever.

"Remember, I have to take Rose's car back to the mall for her. Then I'll come straight back here. I'll be back in just a few minutes, okay?"

"A few minutes . . . okay," Lily parrots, slowly nodding. Naturally, she doesn't question *how* I plan to get back here. Maybe she just thinks I'll walk or run or even sprout wings and fly. And she doesn't question how I got to the mall in the first place. She doesn't even wonder why. It's just not relevant to her at the moment. She trusts that I'll do what I say I'm going to do, and that's that. I've heard our pastor talk about childlike trust and how God wants us all to live like that. In some ways I think Lily's got that one nailed. And sometimes I envy her that. Sometimes I wish my life were that simple. Then I feel guilty for thinking like that. And ungrateful.

"Everything okay?" Rose asks when I hand back her keys.

"Yeah, Lily's home and fine."

"I *mean*, my seat covers."

"Your seat covers are fine too!" Then without thanking her—why should I?—and without saying good-bye, I head for the door. It's all I can do not to growl at her. Then I realize that Rose is similar to Lily in that she wears her selfishness on her sleeve. Well, at least around me. I suppose she's hiding it the rest of the time . . . or trying.

As I walk through the mall, I feel lonelier than ever. I see pairs of girls toting bright-colored shopping bags, or happy couples walking hand in hand, or clusters of teens being loud and obnoxious, and it's painfully clear that I am alone . . . and a misfit. I cannot believe that just a couple of hours ago I was with Owen Swanson, and he acted as if he actually liked me. Did I imagine that?

No, it was real. I know it. But I also know that it's over. Owen got a sneak peak into the life of Aster Flynn today, and even if he was momentarily and unexplainably enchanted, that's all finished and done now. And, really, I can't even blame him. Who wants to pair up with a girl who drags her mentally impaired sister around with her? What kind of guy would put up with someone like Lily hanging around, gawking, saying dumb things, sticking out her chest, making messes?

So it's just as well that this thing—whatever it was—has ended. Chances are, I would've only been hurt worse if it had gone on for a while. I would've really gotten my hopes up—and then been crushed. It's better this way.

I hurry through the mall, eager to get away from a place where I clearly don't belong. I don't even *want* to belong here—expensive clothes, purses, shoes . . . things I obviously can't afford. As I mentioned, I'm more of a Target girl, or "Tar-zhay," as Rose likes to say. And right now I have about ten dollars in my wallet, the remains of the meager allowance I "earn" by helping with Lily. I figured it out once—it's like fifty cents an hour. Slave wages.

As I walk past a wall of store windows curtained off so that a new display can be set up, I notice a girl walking next to me. She's alone too. Her shoulders are slumped, her head is hanging, and she looks like she's carrying the weight of the world on her. And then I realize that's me. That's my reflection.

Eager to escape that pathetic girl, I begin to jog . . . and then I run full speed, bursting out of the mall into the hot afternoon sun. I sprint over to where my bike is still chained to the bike stand. I look at the empty slot where Owen's bike was. Then I hurry to work the combination and unlock my bike. And, although it feels like an inferno now, I pedal like crazy for home.

●   ●   ●

When I get home, I'm dripping with sweat and out of breath. Seriously, I feel like I could be having heatstroke as I fill a glass of water from the faucet and begin to chug it down.

I go to the family room to find Lily flopped down on her old purple beanbag chair and glued to some lame cartoon that's playing on TV.

I stand there trying to determine whether or not I need professional medical attention, but decide that my heart rate seems to be recovering. So I pick up the remote to turn the volume down, which causes Lily to peel her eyes off the TV and look at me with a puzzled expression. "What's a matter with you, Aster?"

"Hot," I gasp.

"Oh." Her brow creases as if she's trying to compute this.

"I just rode my bike all the way from the mall, and it's about a hundred degrees out there."

She frowns and nods like she's taking this in. "Really hot?"

"Really hot." I swipe the cold glass across my forehead, then sink down into the old plaid couch that sags in the middle. Like a hot, sweaty zombie, I sit there and watch *Powerpuff Girls* with Lily. This is my life.

When the show ends, Lily turns to me and says, "Oh yeah. Mom said for you to call her."

"Mom called?" I stand up and reach into my pocket for my cell phone, which I turned off to save the nearly dead battery during my bike ride home. Great. Mom probably tried to call me too. And it's unusual for Mom to call from work, unless something's wrong. "Why did she call?"

"No."

"No?"

"No. She did not call. I called her."

"You called Mom?" Okay, this is definitely not good. Mom does not like to be disturbed at the store unless it's a real honest-to-goodness emergency. It took a long time to get Lily to understand this concept. Once she learned to use the phone, she called Mom again and again, and never for any good reason.

"So why did you call Mom, Lily?" I'm trying to keep my voice calm.

"I wanted to tell her what happened to me."

"You mean about getting your period at the park?"

"Uh-huh."

"But why did you need to call her at work, Lily?" I'm trying not to get mad at her. I know it won't help. "You could've waited until Mom got home to tell her. Remember, you're not supposed to call her at work unless it's an emergency. And then you should always call me first."

"I did."

I nod with realization. "But my phone was off."

"So I got worried. I called Mom."

"What did Mom say?"

"For you to call, *Aster*. Like I told you *already*."

I take in a deep breath and dial O'Leary's. I ask for Mom, and then, seeing that Lily is occupied with another dumb cartoon, I hurry to the bathroom so I can have this conversation in private.

"What is going on there?" my mother demands in a tight voice that's laced with anger.

"Nothing, Mom. Everything's fine. I'm sorry Lily disturbed you."

"She said she was covered in blood and that you had to come and get her."

So I quickly explain, playing it all down. "Then I had to take Rose's car back to her and ride my bike back here and—"

"Wait a minute, Aster. You're saying you rode your bike clear over to the mall, then you borrowed Rose's car to pick up Lily at the park, then you brought her home, drove Rose's car back to the mall, and rode your bike home? Is that right?"

"That's pretty much it."

"Why on earth didn't you just use your bus pass to get Lily?"

So then I have to explain that I was already at the mall when Lily called.

"Why were you at the mall?"

"Why not?" I snap back with irritation.

"Aster!"

"Look, I was riding my bike with a friend. We ended up at the mall, which turned out to be a good thing, because I was able to make it to Lily a lot quicker by driving Rose's car than I would've if I'd had to wait for the bus and then transfer and all that."

"Yes . . . I suppose you're right." Her voice sounds calmer now. I suspect someone has walked into her office, and she doesn't want to sound unprofessional or out of control.

"So, you're not mad?"

"Just worried. Lily sounded so upset. I'm sure that was a humiliating experience for her."

I head back to the family room, where Lily is sprawled out on the floor now. She's eating directly from an oversized bag of chips and spilling crumbs all over our ugly brown carpeting. I notice now that the basket of laundry is still where I put it. Unfolded. She probably forgot. "Lily is perfectly fine," I say in a stiff voice.

Lily looks up at me and grins as if to confirm this.

"I'm sure she's forgotten all about her trauma," I assure Mom.

"Well, I just don't want you to forget your responsibility in regard to your younger sister, Aster."

"Don't worry, Mom. I never do." Although I wish I sometimes could!

"I'll be working late tonight."

"I know." *Of course*, I want to add. *What else is new?* But I know that will sound disrespectful. And I know exactly the response it would provoke. Mom would get very grumpy and say something like, "Well, *someone* has to bring in a living around this place. It's not like your good-for-nothing father is sending us any money lately. You know that he's more than two years behind in child support. If your deadbeat dad would just pay up, I wouldn't have to work so many hours, blah, blah, blah . . ." And so I don't go there. Instead, I tell her to have a good afternoon and to stay cool. Not that it should be a problem since the store has air-conditioning, whereas our house does not.

But here's the honest truth: I think my mom likes working those long hours, and weekends too. I think that work is her way to avoid our *happy home and family life*. Also, I think it's her personal escape hatch—from Lily.

6

I go through the paces of finishing up the laundry, putting things away, and vacuuming Lily's chip mess on the rug. I know I should make her do it, but the last time I tried to get her to vacuum, she sucked up a spoon, which broke the belt, and I had to spend about an hour fixing it. It's just not worth it.

"I'm hungry," she announces at 5:45. "When's dinner?"

"I don't know," I say in a grumpy tone. "Mom's working late, and I don't know when Rose is coming—"

"Rose has a date," Lily informs me. She always loves it when she knows something that someone else doesn't. I think it makes her think she's smarter than she really is.

"How do you know?"

"I heard her talking to her boyfriend on the phone."

"When?"

"Today. Before she went to work." Now Lily gets her sly look. "And I heard Rose say 'I love you too.'"

"You shouldn't eavesdrop."

"I told Kellie about it too. I told Kellie that Rose loves her boyfriend."

"You shouldn't gossip."

"And you know what Kellie said, Aster?"

"No, I don't know what Kellie said." I pick up the last plates from the dishwasher, then slam the door too hard.

"Kellie said that when people love each other, they sometimes get married."

"So?" I put the plates in the cupboard and turn to face Lily. She looks very worried now.

"You think they gonna get married, Aster? You think Rose and Jared will get married?"

"I hope so," I say.

"Why?" Lily demands. "Why you want Rose to get married, Aster?"

"Because then she'll move away, and I can have my own room."

"I don't want Rose to go away." Now Lily looks like she's about to cry, and I feel bad. I know better than to rock her boat. Lily never wants anything to change, not even the sheets on her bed. I'm sure she thinks that life should go on and on just like it is, with the four of us Flynn women living in this cruddy ranch house until we're all old enough to go into a nursing home together.

"Rose isn't going away," I assure Lily. I force a goofy smile. "She's not old enough to get married."

"How old you have to be to get married?"

"I don't know. But older than Rose anyway. Don't worry, Lily. I'm sure Rose is going to be around for a long, long time."

"Oh." Lily nods, seemingly satisfied. "Aster?"

"Huh?"

"I'm hungry."

"Fine. I'll fix you some dinner."

"Okay."

I open the freezer and look at our current selection of Lean Cuisine. Mom got it for herself, then I told her that it would be good for Lily too. Finally we all decided we liked it okay, and it's lots easier than fixing regular dinners. Especially when it's just Lily and me. "How about turkey?"

"Not turkey."

"Beef stroganoff?"

"No. Not that either."

"What then?"

"Lasagna."

It figures. I had been eyeing the lasagna myself. And there's only one package of it. "Fine," I tell her. "Lasagna it is. Now you go watch TV, and I'll fix it."

I take my time in the kitchen. It's nice to have some peace and quiet. As I poke around, I think about Owen. Oh, I know it's hopeless. I know that I had my chance, and now it's over. But I can't help but daydream about what it would be like if Lily hadn't called. Or what it would be like if I was someone else—a normal girl in a normal family with normal friends and a normal life.

This is where my imagination always lets me down. I cannot imagine having a normal life.

• • •

Lily and I eat our Lean Cuisine dinners at the breakfast bar. I insist on this to make for easier cleanup. After we're done, I want to do some drawing, but as soon as I get out my sketchbook and charcoals, Lily insists she must draw too. So I get out her tablet and return to what is turning out to be a pretty good-looking oak tree, but she's still complaining. Her tablet and no. 2 pencil aren't good enough. Even when I let her use my good colored pencils, she's still not happy. But there is no way I'm going to let her use my charcoals and good paper. Not only would that be a waste of expensive supplies, but she'd probably get it all over her. Finally I convince Lily that we should both color together in her *Beauty and the Beast* coloring book.

So my art supplies are safely on top of the fridge, and Lily and I are sitting at the breakfast bar coloring. I'm coloring the teapot, making it very psychedelic, and Lily is giving Beauty a makeover that causes her to resemble the Beast. Maybe it'll help their romance.

The landline rings, and I decide to let it go to the machine since it's probably just a dumb telemarketer, and hearing the machine will make them hang up. But suddenly I hear a guy's voice speaking very politely into the answering machine.

"Hello, this is Owen Swanson, and I'm calling for Aster. I hope this is the right Flynn—"

I snag the phone before Lily can grab it. "Hey," I say as calmly as I can. But now she's standing there staring at me with way too much interest, and I give her the evil eye, meaning *back off, sister!* "This is Aster."

"Hey," he says back. "How are you doing?"

"I'm all right."

"Did everything turn out, uh, okay for your sister?"

"Yeah. She's fine." My cheeks feel warm as I remember how I told him Lily needed "feminine hygiene products." Ugh!

"I felt bad for not being more help. If I had my pickup at the mall, I could've driven you from—"

"It's okay. It all worked out."

"You didn't even get to eat your lunch."

"Oh well." I'm narrowing my eyes at Lily now, trying to appear threatening. But she's not budging, and this stupid phone is the one with a cord, keeping me stuck right here. "Hey, how about if I give you my cell phone number," I say suddenly.

"Yeah, sure, let me grab a pen."

"I mean, then I won't be tying up the landline in case someone's trying to call for, well, you know . . ." Okay, I know I must sound like a complete idiot.

"Okay, I'm ready."

So I tell him my cell number, say a quick good-bye, then run to my room to make sure that I can find my charger. I plug it in, stick my phone in it, then close the bedroom door practically in Lily's face. "Just give me some privacy, okay?"

"Aster's got a boyfriend. Aster's got a boyfriend," she says again and again in her best attempt at a singsong voice, although it comes out in a monotone.

I shove a chair against the door, a trick I learned from Rose since we can't have locks on the doors, thanks to Lily's knack for getting herself locked into places she should be staying out of. My phone rings.

"Hey," I say in a quiet voice.

"Is that better?" Owen asks.

"Yeah. The truth is, I just wanted to escape my snoopy sister."

"Which one?"

I laugh. "Lily."

"Is it rough being the middle child?"

I consider this. "I don't know . . . I mean, I'm pretty sure I wouldn't want Lily to be older than me. And I wouldn't really want to be the oldest one either. Maybe being stuck in the middle's not so bad."

"Well, my brother Wayne is always complaining about being the middle brother. He thinks he misses out on everything."

"So you have another older brother?"

"Yeah. Eric. He's like twenty-three, or is it twenty-four now? About four years older than Wayne."

"Does that make you the baby?"

Owen laughs. "I guess."

And so we talk for a while. Oh, we don't really say much. But I can tell we're trying to get to know each other better. Kind of poking around and seeing how it feels, whether it fits or not.

"Well, I should probably let you go," he finally says, and I realize we've been talking for an hour. My mom will probably be getting home soon, and I haven't helped Lily get ready for bed yet.

"Yeah, maybe so."

"But before you go . . . I was wondering, Aster, would you ever want to go out?"

"Go out?" The pitch of my voice sounds higher.

"You know, on a date, with me."

"Sure." I try to sound calmer than I feel.

"Cool."

"Yeah, cool," I repeat, instantly thinking how dumb that must sound.

"How about Friday?"

"Sure, Friday sounds good." Even as I say this, I know it could be a problem. Rose will probably have a date, and Mom will probably work late. And who will stay with Lily?

"Maybe we could catch a movie or something."

"Yeah. That sounds great." Then we settle on a time and say good-bye. After I hang up, I do the happy dance around the bedroom. But my celebration comes to an end when I realize that I'll have to come up with some kind of a plan for Lily, which might include hiring a babysitter. Well, we've done that before. Not that Lily likes it.

I unwedge the chair from the bedroom door and go out into a strangely quiet house. "Lily?" I call uneasily. Oh no, what if I hurt her feelings and she's gone outside to hide or walk the streets or do something else equally stupid?

"Lily?" I call again. "Where are you?" No answer. Then I go into the kitchen, and to my relief she's there, but her face and hands are covered with dark smudges, almost as if she's planning to do a performance in blackface, which I should warn her is not PC.

Then I see that she's gotten down my art supplies. She's been into my charcoals, which are smeared all over the countertop now. And she's been drawing in my tablet too. What had started out to be a good-looking tree now looks like a black tornado. "Lily!" I scold her. "What have you done?"

"Nothing."

"You got into my things." I now observe that all my charcoals are broken and virtually useless. "You ruined my charcoals!" I shake my finger at her. "You ruined my drawing!"

"No!" she shouts back at me. "I did not!"

So I grab her by the shoulders and drag her over to the mirror that's by the door. "Look at yourself, Lily. You're covered in black. You got into my things!"

Then, just as Lily starts to cry, our mother walks in and stares at us like we're a couple of sideshow freaks. And maybe we are.

"What is going on here?" she asks with highly arched brows.

"Aster being mean!" Lily cries. "She hurting me!"

"I am not. Lily got into my art supplies and made a huge mess."

"I can see that, Aster. But where were you when this happened?"

"Aster was in her bedroom talking to that boy!" Lily shakes her finger at me now. At times like this I think that in a previous life Lily must've been a member of the Gestapo or KGB.

"You have a boy in your bedroom?" my mom asks.

"I was talking on the phone."

Mom just shakes her head. "Well, go help Lily get ready for bed, and you can clean this up later. I'm exhausted."

"Get to the bathroom," I command Lily after Mom disappears to her bedroom at the other end of the house.

"Quit being mean!" Lily shouts.

"You haven't begun to see mean." Then I give her a slight shove toward the direction of the bathroom.

"Don't push me, *Aster*!"

Now, I know that I need to take a deep breath and mentally count to ten or maybe a hundred. I know, I know, I know from years of experience that getting tough with Lily will only make everything much, much worse. Still, I feel so angry at her, not just for messing with my art supplies and making a mess of the counter and herself. I feel like she's messing up my entire life.

"Sorry," I say to her as kindly as I can muster. "It's just that I feel bad that you got into my stuff, Lily. You know how much I like doing art—"

"I like doing art stuff too."

"I know. And we were doing art stuff together, Lily."

67

"But that stupid boy called."

"He's not stupid." I soften my voice again. "Remember that cute boy who gave you a ride to the pool so you could be with your friends?"

"That boy?" She actually seems interested now.

"Yes, that boy. His name is Owen, and he's my friend."

"Your boyfriend?" She gets that mischievous twinkle in her eyes now.

"He's a nice boy, Lily. He's my friend."

"Is he my friend too?"

"Yes, of course. He helped you get to the pool, didn't he?"

She seems to consider this, then nods. "Yes. What's his name?"

"Owen."

"Owen," she repeats as I gently guide her toward the bathroom. She says his name a few times like she's seeing how it feels on her tongue. "Owen. I like that name, Aster."

Then I fix a bath for her and tell her she has ten minutes to get clean. Fortunately, this is something that Lily can do for herself, for the most part anyway. "And don't get your hair wet," I remind her. Then, just for good measure, I soap up a washcloth and hand it to her. "And get all that yucky black stuff off of your pretty face, okay?"

"Okay," she chirps back at me. She loves it when I call her pretty.

"I'll get your pj's and be right back."

Her ten minutes stretch into about twenty. But finally we've gone through all the regular bedtime routine, and she's tucked into bed and ready for prayers.

"Dear heavenly Father," she begins just like usual. "Bless Mommy. Bless Rose. Bless Aster. And bless Owen!"

This makes me laugh.

"Why that funny?"

"It's not funny, Lily. It's just sweet that you remembered Owen."

"He's our friend."

I nod. "Yes, he is."

Lily continues her prayer. She says she's sorry for a couple of incidents that must've happened at the pool or the park, and she also says she's sorry for getting into my art stuff. "And help me be a good girl," she says finally. "And help Micah to be my friend. I don't mean boyfriend, God. I just want him to hold my hand sometimes. Amen."

"Who is Micah?" I ask as I pull the sheet up around her chin the way she likes it. Even though it's still pretty warm in the house, Lily likes to have her covers on.

"The new boy."

"Does he go to the rec center?"

"Yes."

"Is he nice?"

"Yes. But he doesn't want to hold my hand."

"Why not?"

She wrinkles her nose. "He says I have girl germs."

I laugh. "Well, just tell him he has boy germs."

"Does he?"

I shrug. "I guess."

"Maybe I don't wanna hold his hand."

"Maybe not." I turn on her Winnie the Pooh night-light and turn off the overhead one. "Good night, Princess Lily."

"Good night, Princess Aster." She giggles over our old good night game. I haven't called her Princess in ages. "I love you!"

"I love you too," I say. "And I'm sorry I got mad at you."

"That's okay."

And as I close her door, leaving it cracked open the prerequisite six inches, I realize that she means it. It *is* okay. She has forgiven me. But when I go to the kitchen, begin cleaning up the mess she made, and toss my ruined charcoals into the trash, I'm not so sure that I have totally forgiven her.

7

I have less than two days to figure this out. How can I go out with Owen on Friday night and still be sure that Lily is taken care of? I know I can't count on Mom. She almost always works late on Friday nights. In desperation, I decide to ask Rose. She's been out with Jared again. Not only is it past her curfew, since it's after midnight, but I can tell she's been drinking too. And I actually think if I'm just desperate enough that I might use this evidence against her. Am I above blackmail? Maybe not . . . not when it comes to my second chance with Owen.

But after I nicely ask Rose about staying home with Lily, she just laughs in my face, then says, "Yeah, right."

"Why not?" I plead.

"Because I'm going out with Jared, that's why not." She pulls her shirt off and throws it onto the floor with the rest of her slush pile.

"You could invite Jared over here, and you guys could—"

"Like *that's* going to happen."

71

"But I need a break, Rose. I take care of Lily *all* the time. 24-7."

"She goes to the rec center during the day."

"Yeah, but who gets her to the rec center? Who picks her up? Who is constantly on call for her? Who feeds her and stays with her and puts her to bed?"

"Poor little you."

"I'm not asking for sympathy. Just some help."

"Well, here's my help for you, Aster. Let me give you a bit of advice."

"Huh?"

"Tell Mom to find someone to take care of Lily or to take care of her herself—period. How simple is that?" She staggers slightly as she leans forward to make her point.

"Yeah, right."

"See!" She shakes her head like I'm this hopeless case. "That's your problem, Aster. You are such a pushover. You let Mom and Lily walk all over you." She kicks off her shoes and walks around like she's imitating them.

And you too, I want to add. *You walk on me too.*

"You just need to learn to say no."

"Just say no. Yeah, that's going to work."

"Hey, you're not Mom's slave. You're almost seventeen, and you've never even been on a date. And I'll tell you what, if you keep letting them push you around, you never will go on a date either. You'll grow up to be an old maid, taking care of Mom and Lily for the rest of your life." She laughs like that's real funny. "You know why I draw the line like I do?"

"Because you're mean and selfish?"

"Get a clue, little girl. I learned this one early: no one is looking out for you but *you*."

I bite my lower lip. As horrid as that sounds, it sure does feel accurate. Then I remember something. "God is looking out for me." I hold my head a little higher now. How can she dispute that?

But she just gets this smug little smile. "Well, if the big guy's looking out for you, he's sure doing a bang-up job of it. Man, with friends like that, who needs—"

"Oh, shut up!" I yell as I walk out of our room and into the darkened living room. Then, as I sit out there by myself, I can't help but think about what she said. Not about God so much. But about how I need to look after myself because no one else will. I hate to admit it, but I do think she's right. Still, I want to believe that God is taking care of me too—that's been my lifeline at times. And so I pray.

"Dear God," I whisper so quietly that even if anyone in my family was listening, which isn't likely, they wouldn't really hear. "I feel so trapped. I do believe you're looking out for me. But my life sure doesn't seem to get better. And all I want is a little slice of the normal pie. Can't you please help me to figure something out so that I can have a life?" I pray some more, remembering to thank him for all the good things (I don't want to seem ungrateful), and then I say "Amen" and tiptoe to bed.

As I lie there, I think about Owen. I imagine him as my prince driving up in his big white pickup and taking me away from here—forever! Okay, I'm fully aware that that's dumb. But, hey, it's my daydream!

● ● ●

On Thursday, after I get Lily to the rec center, I call Crystal. I can hear the surprise in her voice since I hardly ever call her like this—just out of the blue.

"What's up?" I ask.

"Not much. Can you believe how hot it is?"

"Yeah, especially for June." So I take this as my opportunity to tell her about my bike ride with Owen yesterday.

"No way," she says loudly.

"Way," I insist.

"You went on a bike ride with Owen Swanson? Just like that?"

"Just like that."

"Are you making this up?"

"No, honest, Crystal." So then I tell her the rest of the story, how he got Lily to the pool, then how Lily ruined our lunch . . . and everything.

"Oh, that's too bad."

"Yeah, I was pretty bummed."

"But maybe it was for the best."

74

"Huh?"

"Oh, you know, Owen's kind of got a reputation."

"For doing what?" Okay, I'm not dumb, I've heard rumors. But what if they were just that—rumors?

"You know, with the girls. He's gone with every popular girl in school."

"Meaning?"

"Meaning that you shouldn't be too disappointed if he's not interested in you."

"How do you know he's *not* interested?"

"Well, I just assumed . . . and I don't want to see you get hurt."

"Maybe I *won't* get hurt." It's taking all of my self-control not to just blast her with my news. But I have a feeling I need to play my cards carefully. Especially if I'm going to get her help. And I need her help.

"It's just that you don't really expect someone like Owen Swanson to be . . . well, you know . . . serious about you."

Part of me is seriously indignant now, but I know I need to keep my cool if I'm going to ask this huge favor. "Yeah, that's kind of what I thought too. I mean, hey, we had a nice bike ride. No big deal, right?"

"Exactly."

"But then he called me last night, Crystal. We talked for an hour!"

"No way!" she shrieks so loudly that I have to hold the phone away from my ear.

"Way!" I say back at her.

"You talked *for an hour*?"

Okay, I'm thinking this almost feels like a best friend conversation now. Maybe I've underestimated Crystal. "Yeah, it was so awesome. I mean, we all think Owen is Mr. I'm-So-Cool, and it turns out he's really just a regular guy. He even remembered me from grade school. He said he thought I was cute and good at sports."

"Yeah?"

I'm tempted to tell her the line about "Where have you been all my life?" but I want to keep that one special, something that's just between Owen and me. "Anyway, I don't really know where it's going, but here's the coolest part. He asked me out on Friday."

"Really?"

"Yeah."

"Wow."

"I know . . ." I lean back into the couch and sigh. *"Wow."*

"So are you going out?"

"Sure."

"Oh." Something about the way she says "oh" sounds unsure. Like maybe she thinks it's not such a good idea. Or she's going to lecture me about his reputation again.

"Why?" I ask. "Do you think I should've turned him down?"

"Oh . . . I don't know."

"What?"

"Well, I just wondered . . . I mean, Owen isn't like us, and he hangs with a pretty wild crowd. And you're a Christian, Aster."

"So?"

"So how are you going to fit in with his friends—you know, the partying types?"

"I'm not dating his friends."

"Not exactly, but it'll be a factor . . . and sooner or later there could be other problems too. You know what they say about being unequally yoked."

"It's not like we're getting married, Crystal. And, really, Owen doesn't seem like that to me. Not when you really get to know him." Of course, I feel both offended and defensive now. What right does she have to dis my boyfriend? Okay, he's not really my boyfriend. Not yet anyway. But why is she being so judgmental?

"How well do you really know Owen?" she demands.

"Huh?"

"Wasn't yesterday the first time you actually talked to him?"

"Sort of . . ."

"So how well do you know him?"

"Well enough to know that I can trust him."

Now she doesn't say anything, but I suspect she has a skeptical look on her face. Whatever.

"Anyway, Crystal, how can I get to know him if I don't spend time with him?"

"Good point."

I decide to play the Christian card on her now. "Besides, as Christians, we're not supposed to judge people, right?"

"Well . . . we're supposed to have discernment."

"And, as Christians," I continue, disregarding her discernment comment and whatever that's supposed to mean, "aren't we supposed to be reaching out to others?"

"You mean like dating for Jesus?"

"Funny."

"Well, I've heard it's not a good way to witness."

Suddenly I wonder why I even called her. Oh yeah, I wanted to get her to help me with Lily. "Anyway, Crystal, I'm sure you're busy, so let me cut to the chase."

"What chase?"

"Well, as you know, I kinda take care of Lily. And my mom works on Friday nights, and Rose is going out, so I was wondering if—"

"Please don't ask me to babysit Lily for you."

"It would be such a huge, enormous favor, Crystal. I would owe you—"

"Don't you remember the last time I babysat Lily?"

"Yes, but she didn't know you very well, and she was having a bad day—"

"She locked me out of the house and called 9-1-1, Aster. Do you know how embarrassing it was when the cops showed up, and I had to explain in detail that I hadn't beaten or molested her, or whatever it was she told them I'd done? I've never been so humiliated."

"But that was a couple of years ago, Crystal. Can't you give her one more chance? Lily likes you now."

"Humph."

Only someone like Crystal or me would say "humph." I guess we really are nerds.

"What would Jesus do?" I finally ask. This is my trump card, my trumpiest trump card, and I'm praying it will work.

"I'll tell you what, I'll pray about it. I'll ask Jesus to tell me what to do. How's that?"

I sigh. "Well, I guess if that's the best you—"

"That's all you're getting from me today, Aster. Besides, what if Jesus doesn't want you to go out with Owen Swanson? Have you thought about that?"

It's all I can do not to just hang up. But then I know she'd refuse to Lily-sit for me. So I bite my tongue.

"Sorry," she says. "I don't want to sound mean. But I do hope you're being smart about this."

What is it with Crystal? It's like some nosy sixty-year-old body-snatching woman has taken over this girl's mind. "Don't be such a worrywart, Crystal. I'm not marrying the boy, we're just going to a movie, okay?"

"Well, don't blame me if it goes wrong."

"I won't." Now I realize I need to sweeten this up. "And, really, I do appreciate your concern. In fact, it would be cool if you were here at my house when Owen picks me up. That way you could see for yourself that he's totally tame."

"And then I get stuck with Lily for the evening?"

"You make Lily sound like a monster, Crystal. She's actually a very sweet girl. She just needs a lot of love, but if you can't handle it . . ."

"I'll get back to you on it, okay?"

"Thanks, Crystal. I really appreciate it."

I hang up, cross my fingers, and even say a brief prayer. "Please, God, have mercy on me. I need a break. Amen."

8

Amazingly, Friday morning goes way smoother than usual. Lily is actually very cooperative and cheerful as we go through the paces of getting her ready. By ten o'clock she is safely at the rec center, and I now have six blissful hours to myself.

"Morning," the mailman says as our paths cross in front of my house. Then he hands me a small pile of envelopes, which look like bills and will put my mom in her regular monthly mood. And I'm not talking PMS. But I thank him and take them into the house. I toss the junk and then notice that one of the long and thin white envelopes is addressed to me. But then I see the high school's return address and Ms. Grieves's name, and I'm tempted to throw it away.

Ms. Grieves is a guidance counselor, and I'm pretty sure she thinks I'm her big charity case. During the last month of school, she invited me to meet all the visiting college reps and fill out all kinds of applications for financial aid and scholarships and who knows what else. I complied simply to placate the woman and hopefully get her off my case. But it's summer break, for Pete's sake. You'd think she'd quit riding me for a month or two.

I reluctantly open the envelope and remove the neatly printed letter. Fortunately, it looks like a form letter. Maybe she's taken on more charity cases besides me. One can only hope. The letter is another invitation to yet another college recruitment event. What's the deal? Are colleges that desperate for students these days? Enrollment falling? Whatever the case, I am not going to Ms. Grieves's little soiree. I toss the letter in the trash and head to the kitchen to clean up the breakfast things. College for me will probably end up being LCC too. Or, if I'm lucky, maybe the university.

But I don't need to think about that today. All I can think about today is whether or not Crystal will recognize that her Christian duty is to come to the aid of a needy friend. I'd call her, but I know it's too early. Crystal, like most other normal teens, doesn't get up until about noon during the summer. I can't even imagine what it would be like to sleep that late. Lily has always been an early riser.

Then I remember that Owen was up bright and early the other day. Okay, it was around ten, but still he seemed wide awake. Maybe he's an early riser too. Maybe he'll be rolling through my neighborhood again this morning, on his way to . . . where? Who cares?

I do a quick personal cleanup and brush my teeth. I put on a fresh shirt, some lip gloss, and mascara, then grab my sketch pad and a pencil and dash out the door. I sit on the front steps and attempt to appear absorbed in a drawing, but I'm actually peering up and down the street, trying to spy a shiny white pickup that just happens to drive by. Except that it's not driving by. And this troubles me, although I realize that's ridiculous. Almost as ridiculous as me sitting out here pretending to sketch.

So I go back inside, wander around, and wish that my phone would ring. It doesn't. So then I decide to figure out what I'll wear on my Big Date (you know, the power of positive thinking). But after I stand in front of my pathetic section of closet for about ten minutes, I realize that my wardrobe really is sad, and I'm actually tempted to ride the bus to the mall and beg a loan from Rose so that I can do some shopping. But then I realize how stupid that is. Not to mention shallow. And, really, it's not who I am. So why should I go there?

Finally, in an effort to distract myself, I pick up the latest Jane Austen book that I've been reading. I'm fully aware that it's somewhat nerdish for a teen to be reading Austen, but she was on the recommended reading list in my AP English lit class. So I picked up *Emma*, and after I got over the old-fashioned and sometimes bulky language, I was totally hooked. Even though Jane Austen lived like three centuries ago, I can relate to her. After that, I read *Sense and Sensibility* and *Mansfield Park*, and now I'm about a fourth of the way through *Pride and Prejudice*.

Fortunately, these books are available at the public library, and since Lily loves to go there for Saturday story hour, it's a cheap and easy form of entertainment for both of us. And I suppose, if I am perfectly honest, reading has always been a handy escape for me. I get to run away from my dreary little life for a few hours. Of course, Rose thinks I'm nuts. She can't believe that I read because I want to. She says it's a waste of time. But then, that's Rose.

Up until now I thought that *Emma* was my favorite Austen book, perhaps because it was my first. But now I'm thinking *Pride and Prejudice* may top it. Primarily because the story involves five sisters, three of whom remind me a tiny bit of me and my siblings—or maybe I'm just reading a whole lot more into it. But it's interesting that I relate to the second-oldest sister, Elizabeth. And the sister most like Rose is the youngest sister, Lydia. She's a real piece of work. I'm not sure where Lily fits—in spirit she's sweet like Jane, the oldest sister, but Jane is pretty and smart, albeit a bit naive.

Anyway, it should be interesting to see how the story develops. I will state, however, that Owen is nothing like that snooty Mr. Darcy, who goes around snubbing everyone, even Elizabeth. But knowing Jane Austen from her previous books, I suspect she will redeem the snob in the end. Although I doubt that she will make me like him.

Suddenly I'm interrupted by the ringing of my phone. I'm hoping it's not Lily with another disaster. I packed several sanitary pads and even a couple of Advil in her backpack in case she gets cramps, although she rarely does. To my relief, it's Crystal.

"Hey, Crystal," I say in a cheerful voice.

"Hey, Aster." Her voice is flat-sounding, and I suspect the worst.

"What's up?"

"Okay," she says, "I'll do it."

"You will?"

"Yes. But if Lily pulls a stunt, I swear I will never do it again."

"She won't," I promise. "I'll do everything I can to have her ready for this. In fact, it might help if you came over early, and we can all just hang out like friends. I'll have Lily's favorite foods here. I'll even rent the latest *Shrek* movie. She adores Shrek. And I'll have everything all ready for her bedtime. We can pretend it's a slumber party."

"Yeah, right."

"Your enthusiasm is underwhelming."

"Sorry. But this is a sacrifice, Aster. I hope you appreciate it."

"I totally do!"

So we arrange for Crystal to come over after four. And suddenly I'm feeling freaked over this whole thing. I mean, I'm *really* going out with Owen now. It's no longer just a daydream fantasy where I control the outcome. This is for real.

I go back and stand in front of the closet again. I'm so desperate I even look at Rose's clothes—and she would kill me if I touched a single thing of hers. Then I tell myself I'm being shallow. But it's not working for me this time. Maybe I *want* to be shallow. Good grief, I'm nearly seventeen. If I can't be shallow now, when can I?

Once again, I consider going to Rose for help. But then I know Rose. If she thinks that she's helping, she'll want to take over. She'll want to pick out what I'll wear on my Big Date, and she'll probably want to give me a whole makeover. No way am I going there.

Then I realize that it's almost the weekend, and Mom always gives me my allowance on Saturday. I know she hates it when I ask for an advance, and I rarely do. But maybe it's worth it to ask. After all, she is my mom. Why shouldn't she want to help me have a life? Seriously!

But instead of calling her, which she hates, I ride my bike downtown and wait until it's three minutes past noon. Then I go in and find her in her office, getting ready to go have lunch.

"What are you doing here?" she asks with worried eyes.

"Just stopping in to say hi."

Now she looks suspicious. "Hello."

I know it's time to humble myself and make my request, but part of me wants to turn and just leave. Forget that "she's my mother" nonsense. Maybe it doesn't matter.

"Well, what is it, Aster?" she persists. "I'm supposed to meet the girls at the café. Marie is ordering for me."

So I quickly spill my story about how I rode bikes with Owen, how he asked me to a movie, and how I've even got Crystal coming to stay with Lily.

"Crystal?" Mom looks wary. She probably remembers the last fiasco.

"I'll make sure that everything is cool," I assure her. "Lily knows Crystal now. And she likes her. Crystal will come early, and I'll have Lily's favorite foods and movie. It'll be like a slumber party."

Mom seems to consider this and finally nods. "Seems you've got everything covered, Aster."

"Except that I'm kind of broke, and I wondered if I could get my allowance a day early. I mean, I need to rent Lily a movie and get some—"

"Well, why didn't you just say you came for money in the first place?"

"I, uh, I . . ."

She opens her purse, pulls out two twenties, and hands them to me. "Here you go."

"Thanks, Mom." I smile at her. This was easier than I expected.

Now she actually smiles. "Thank you, Aster. You do a wonderful job taking care of Lily. I really do appreciate it."

I blink in surprise. "Well . . . thanks." I'm not used to this kind of praise.

"Now, if you don't mind, I better run."

"Not at all." I stay in her office, watching as she heads out. As usual, she's well dressed in a neat, cream-colored pantsuit. Not that she wears designer or expensive clothes. But respectably nice, like a store manager.

I remember once when Rose questioned why Mom always got to have new clothes, and Mom explained that it was a working expense and that the store gave her a discount. I thought it made sense, but Rose wasn't buying. She was just plain jealous. Not long after that, Rose got a job and started buying her own clothes and things. For a while Lily and I got her hand-me-downs, but then I got taller and Lily got fatter, and Rose started holding on to everything tighter.

Less than fifty bucks to buy some "date" clothes, rent a movie, get Lily some junk food, and have enough money left for the next week might seem a challenge to some people, but I've learned over time how to shop smart. So I give myself a budget and head over to Retro Reruns, a thrift store where I sometimes get lucky. Although I learned in middle school never to buy anything that's too unusual, particularly something that's handmade.

There's a saying that "familiarity breeds contempt," and I discovered that for myself when I purchased a pale blue dress at St. Vincent's and wore it to eighth grade graduation. It turned out to have been owned previously by Amanda Kerr, and she was furious when she saw me in it. It seemed her grandmother had sewn it for her, and she didn't even know her mother had given it away. At one point I almost thought Amanda was going to tear that pretty dress right off me. Naturally, I never wore it again. And I never made that mistake again either. Now I buy only used clothes that I know I might've gotten new. I prefer ones with labels from Gap and Banana Republic, and one time I got lucky and found a pair of Lucky jeans. But I avoid anything unusual or distinct, including big designer names that are still fairly expensive, even for a thrift store.

"Hey, Aster," says Beth, a salesclerk who's befriended me this past year. She attends a community college but wants to go to design school someday. "Long time no see."

"How's it going?"

"Kinda slow. What are you looking for?"

I casually explain that I'm going out and wanted something new, trying to act like it was no big deal.

"So . . . you have a boyfriend now?"

"Not exactly. I mean, it's our first date."

"But you really like him?"

"I guess." What an understatement, but I suppose I'm trying to protect my pride—in case it all goes sideways again.

"Well, I have just the thing, and it'll look awesome on you." I follow her to a rack where she digs around until she pulls out this very cool, totally retro, and, unfortunately, too-unique top. She holds it up and smiles. "What do you think?"

I sort of frown. "It's fantastic, Beth. But it's too, well, you know, too one of a kind."

She laughs. "You're afraid you'll wear it and the original owner will walk up and make a scene?"

"Exactly."

"Well, you're looking at the original owner."

"This was yours?"

"Actually, it was my mom's back in the seventies. She saved it, and I did some more work on it, but it's a little too small for me." She points to her well-endowed chest and shrugs. "So I decided to sell it."

Now I look at the tag to see she's marked it at $25, which is a little more than I planned to spend. And yet this top is so cool. "It was really yours?"

"Would I lie to you?"

I can tell by her face that she wouldn't. Still, I'm a little uneasy about the price.

"Go try it on, Aster. See if it's not perfect."

So I go back to the funky, cool dressing room that's made from a bunch of Indian saris hung around some kind of hula hoop ring. The shirt's fabric is an assortment of gauzy patches and lots of embroidery and beads and things. And when I have it on, I come out to look in the big mirror and am amazed. "Wow."

"It's magical, isn't it?"

"Very cool."

"And since it's you, Aster, I'm reducing the price to $20. But this is a onetime-only offer."

"Sold."

"And if you can spare that extra five bucks, we've got some very cool espadrilles that I'm thinking are your size. Aren't you about a nine?"

"Yeah. But what are espadrilles?" It sounds like some kind of Mexican food, which reminds me that I'm hungry.

Beth produces an amazing pair of lacy canvas wedges with strings that tie around your ankle. I try them on and walk around a bit, and Beth whistles. "You look fabulous, dahling."

"Really, you think the shirt and shoes go with my shorts?" I have on my khaki shorts.

"I think a little denim skirt would be nicer."

"You sound just like a salesman."

"Aster, this is your *lucky* day." She grins.

"Lucky as in Lucky?"

"Yep. An adorable skirt came in last week, probably your size too."

Lucky jeans are fairly common, but a skirt might be recognizable. I'm feeling a little wary. "Did you see who consigned it?"

"Yeah, it was a gal in her twenties. She's moving to the East Coast and needed some cash."

By the time I leave Retro Reruns, I've gone over my budget. I still have enough money left for Lily's DVD and junk food, but next week is going to be tight. Plus, I didn't ask Crystal if she expects me to pay her for babysitting or if it's a favor for a friend. Maybe I can write her an IOU. But I'm thinking that if I really want to have a life and start dating and wearing cool threads, well, I might need to come up with a way to make more money.

I park my bike in the garage, which still needs cleaning, then carry my precious bag of "new" clothes into the house.

Suddenly I feel mad. Or maybe I feel torn. I mean, on one hand, I'm jazzed that I was able to get such a cool outfit, but I'm thinking about money—rather my lack of it—and I wonder if Rose might be right. Maybe Mom is taking advantage of me. Seriously, who else could Mom get to do all that I do for Lily for forty bucks a week? I doubt that anyone would even do it for forty bucks a day. Maybe it really is time to ask for a raise.

9

"Well, don't you look . . . uh, *interesting*." Rose says this with one brow lifted awkwardly. This is her attempt to mimic Vivien Leigh playing Scarlett O'Hara in *Gone with the Wind*. Rose relates well to Scarlett, but I think Scarlett was extremely selfish and self-centered—guess that works for Rose too.

"If that's supposed to be a compliment, you might want to work on your delivery."

"Ooh, aren't we clever with our fancy words." Rose makes her hoity-toity face now. This is her usual reaction to any of my attempts to be witty. "But seriously, Aster, where did you get that weird shirt? Is it *used*?"

She says the word "used" as if she's saying "soiled" or "grotesque" or "nasty." But I try not to take offense. What would be the point?

"It's *retro*, Rose."

She snorts a laugh. "Yeah, right. Retro's just another word for Goodwill and Salvation Army stores."

"Whatever." I so don't want to get into a fight with her. Not just because I'm trying to get ready for my Big Date, but because a fight with Rose could be the undoing of Lily. And, at the moment, Lily is doing so well.

It's a little past six o'clock, and Rose popped home for just enough time to change her outfit for her date with Jared. Hopefully, she'll leave as quickly as she came. Right now Crystal and Lily are in the family room playing Candyland. And I must hand it to Crystal, she's being a good sport and really trying. They were getting along so well that I thought this might be my best chance to get ready for my Big Date. Then Rose showed up.

I lace up one of my espadrilles and tie the strings in back just how Beth showed me. I even shaved my legs and put lotion on after my shopping expedition. No, not for the skanky reason that movies and TV toss about. I shaved my legs for these shoes, which I must admit really are spectacular. I've never had a pair of wedge heels before, and I've been practicing walking in them since I got home.

Before I can put on the other shoe, Rose has picked it up and seems to be examining it. I brace myself for her next scathing "used" comment.

"Where did you get these?"

"Does it matter?"

"Yeah, it does."

"Why?" Suddenly I'm worried that they might've been hers and she's going to flip out on me, but then I remember she's still a size eight.

"Because these are Stuart Weitzman."

"Who's he? And why would he wear girl shoes?"

She laughs, then frowns. "You don't know what I'm talking about, do you? Stuart Weitzman is a shoe designer."

Suddenly I do remember a weird name on the label, but then I never pay attention to labels. Why should I? "So?"

"These are Stuart Weitzman shoes, Aster. They must've cost a fortune. *Where* did you get them?" Now she's looking at me like she thinks I walked in with a shotgun and robbed some fancy designer shoe store, not that I even know where one is located.

"I already told you," I say coolly. "Retro Reruns. They carry all sorts of designer stuff. I just got them because they were cute."

She tosses me my shoe now. "Well, I'll be . . . my fashion-challenged little sister is developing designer taste." She laughs. "In that case you better get yourself a real job or a sugar daddy."

I don't even look up or respond to this potentially volatile suggestion. I simply lace up my shoe, then stand up and force a smile. For Crystal and Lily's sake, which is ultimately for my sake, I will be civilized to Rose. "Or maybe I'll just keep shopping thrift shops and save tons of money."

She frowns. "Don't you wonder whose feet were in those shoes, Aster?"

"Not particularly." I give my hair a quick second glance in the mirror. I decided to wear it down with just a bit of it pulled back to keep it away from my face. Still, I'm not quite comfortable going out with this huge mane of hair.

"What if she had athlete's foot?"

"Huh?" I look back at Rose, trying to remember what she's babbling about.

"The person whose shoes you're wearing."

I stick out a foot, admiring how fantastic the shoes look and still slightly surprised at how long my legs are. I'm thankful that Owen is tall. "These are my shoes, Rose. I paid for them myself."

She makes a harrumph sort of noise, and I must say it's unbecoming. I tell her to have a nice evening, then go out to check on Lily and Crystal.

"It's my turn," Lily is insisting.

"No," Crystal says. "You don't get a second turn this time."

"Hey," I say as I get down on my knees next to Lily. I send Crystal what I hope is a visual clue with my eyes. "I think it *is* Lily's turn. See?" I point to her marker as if that explains everything. The truth is, Lily cheats. And I let her. It's just easier that way.

Crystal looks slightly confused, then quickly nods as if she gets it. "Oh yeah, I guess you're right. Go ahead, Lily."

"See?" Lily says with satisfaction. She takes a card and moves her marker to the lollipop space, then turns and frowns at me. "Why are you dressed like that?"

"Like what?"

"Fancy."

I kind of shrug. "I'm not fancy." Then I stand up and go sit on the couch. Lily follows me with an expression that I can only describe as suspicious.

"What you doing, *Aster*?"

"Sitting on the couch." I smile at her. "Hey, it's almost time to watch *Shrek*."

This distracts her, and she claps her hands in delight. "*Shrek*! *Shrek*! We're gonna watch *Shrek*!"

"But we have to finish our game, don't we?" Crystal says. "I mean, after all, you are winning, Lily."

"Oh yeah," Lily says. "I am winning."

While they return to their game, I make two bags of microwave popcorn and pour them into a big bowl. Then I get out several cans of soda and pour a bag of Reese's Pieces into Lily's favorite pink bowl. I put all this on a tray and carry it out to the family room.

"Wow," Rose says. She's standing over Crystal and Lily now. "Looks like you girls are having quite the party."

"A slumber party," Lily proclaims proudly.

"That's nice of Crystal to babysit you."

Lily scowls up at Rose. "Crystal is not babysitting me, *Rose*!"

"That's right," Crystal says quickly. "We're friends. I'm here for the slumber party."

Now Rose laughs. "Yeah, whatever." Then, as usual, she walks away, and I'm left to pick up the pieces.

"You're right," I tell Lily. "Crystal is *not* a babysitter. There are no babies here, right?"

"Right." But Lily is still scowling.

"This is a slumber party," Crystal says. "We're going to watch *Shrek* and eat junk food."

"Yeah," I say as I go over to put the DVD into the machine and get it ready to go. "This is girlfriends just hanging together and having fun." I can hear Jared's voice in the living room now, followed by the sound of the front door closing. It takes all my self-control not to shout, "Good riddance!" Sometimes I feel like I could kill Rose. Not literally. But sometimes she makes me crazy.

● ● ●

Soon we're all settled into the beginning of the movie. I watch the clock, counting each minute like it's my last and actually praying that this will go smoothly. Despite Rose's attempt at sabotage, Lily is into the movie now. She's junking out and almost doesn't seem to notice whether I'm here or not. My plan is to simply slip away without making a big deal. I think it will be easier on everyone that way. Lily will probably assume I'm in the bathroom or kitchen. And she'll be so absorbed by the movie that she should be fine. By the time the movie ends, my mom will be getting home, and Crystal will be free to go. We've got it all worked out.

I give Crystal a little nod as in *hint hint.* "I'm going to the bathroom," I announce. Lily doesn't even look up from her beanbag chair. I go toward the hallway, then detour into the living room, where I keep one eye on the driveway and one toward the family room.

Finally I see a familiar white pickup pull in. Before Owen

is out of his truck, before he can come to the door, I quietly open the door and slip out.

I am free! Gloriously, wonderfully, amazingly free! I want to dance and sing and shout. But I simply smile at Owen, who is halfway up the walk now. I explain that, for Lily's benefit, I had to sort of sneak out.

"Oh yeah," he says quietly. "No problem."

"My friend Crystal is babysitting—no, not babysitting." I correct myself as Owen opens the passenger door for me. "Lily is *not* a baby. Anyway, everything is cool, and Lily is going to be just fine."

His eyes light up as he helps me into the cab. "And you are *looking* just fine."

"Thanks."

"So, just relax, okay?"

I kind of laugh as I get in. "You must think I'm neurotic."

"I think you obsess over your sister. And that you need a break."

As he closes the door, I tell myself to forget about Lily now. She will be fine. Crystal will be fine. This is my night for freedom, and I intend to enjoy it to the max.

"You really do look pretty tonight, Aster." Owen starts his engine and backs out.

"Well, thanks." I smooth my skirt, which is a little on the short side, but Beth told me it looked great. "Shoot, girl, with legs like yours," she said, "why not?" Even so, I'm not so sure.

Owen is good at making small talk. Socially comfortable. And I pretend that I am too. Still, I feel a little over my head right now. Like what made me think I can pull this off? It turns out the movie he wants to see (I tell him I want to see it too, although it's sci-fi and not my favorite genre) doesn't start until nearly nine. "Are you hungry?" he asks.

"Yeah, a little." Okay, that's an understatement. I had an apple for lunch, then a few bites of popcorn and some Reese's Pieces, which are sitting like rocks at the pit of my stomach. I am starving.

"I was thinking about how you didn't get to eat your lunch the other day," he says, "and how we both like Greek. Want to go to Anatole's?"

"Seriously?"

"Why not?"

"Just that it's a really cool place to eat." I actually have never been there, but I've heard it's awesome. "But don't you need reservations?"

He gives me a quick grin. "As a matter of fact, you do."

"Did you?"

"Uh-huh."

Okay, this is feeling like a real date. I mean, it is a real date. But dinner at Anatole's and a movie. How much more date-like can you get?

"Wow, that sounds great," I say.

● ● ●

So it is that I find myself in one of our town's better restaurants, sharing falafel mezes (*meze* is Greek for "appetizer") with Owen. Next we have Caesar salads, followed by moussaka and gyros. Everything is amazing, or else I'm just so ravenous that I would eat wood. No, it's amazing.

We finish off with baklava and some very strong coffee. I'm not really a coffee drinker, but this is a night for new things, right?

"My grandma was Greek," Owen says. "She used to make baklava too."

"Used to?"

"She died when I was fifteen." He forks a piece of the flaky crust. "I still haven't found anyone who can make it as good as hers." Then he goes on to explain how she would let him help her roll out dozens of paper-thin sheets of phyllo dough on a big marble slab. "Then we'd drape these sheets all over the place, over her tables and chairs, like we were hanging up the laundry, except it was pastry. Then she'd layer all those sheets into a huge pan with syrup, spices, and nuts and things." He smacks his lips. "Really good."

"This is good too," I say.

He nods. "Yeah, it is."

Okay, I know I'm too young to fall in love. Really, I am. But I sure do like this guy. Hearing him talk about his grandma, how they made baklava together—well, it's very charming, very endearing, and slightly mind-boggling. I wonder what Crystal would think if she knew he was like this. But then I think I don't want to tell her—I want to keep some of these tasty little morsels to myself. Of course, thinking of Crystal only makes me think of Lily, and I can't help but glance at my watch and feel anxious. *Please, let it be going well.*

"You okay?" Owen asks.

I look up. "Sorry. I was thinking about Lily and hoping everything's okay at home." Then, whether it was stupid or not, I actually tell him about the other time Crystal stayed with Lily and how she got locked out and questioned by the police. But Owen simply laughs at this story, and I realize it doesn't hurt to be honest about my life. After all, I am who I am. It's not like I can hide anything. Not with a family like mine. Why try?

I feel like God is smiling down on me as we leave the restaurant and walk across the parking lot to Owen's pickup. It's one of those perfect summer evenings. The air is still warm and luxurious against your skin, and the sky is rosy pink, the way it gets just before the sunset. Even the Greek music being piped out into the parking lot is enticing.

For the second time tonight, I feel like throwing up my arms and dancing. Then, to my stunned amazement, I actually do. Kind of a little Greek happy dance. Owen laughs, but being a good sport, he even attempts to dance with me, although we kind of stumble around, and I actually step on his foot.

"Sorry," I say as he helps me into the pickup. "I couldn't help myself."

"Hey, I thought that was totally cool."

102

"It's just that freedom like this . . . well, it's kind of intoxicating."

He throws back his head and laughs loudly. "And to think the rest of us just take it for granted." Now he has both hands planted on either side of the opening for the passenger door, he's leaning forward ever so slightly, and I'm almost worried that he's going to kiss me. Instead, he slowly shakes his head like he's amazed. "Man, Aster, I just don't know how you do it."

"Do what?" I look at him curiously.

"You know, take care of your sister like you do."

"Oh . . ." I think I'd almost forgotten about Lily just then. "I guess it's like the old Nike saying. I just do it."

He nods, then closes my door, and I find myself sitting there thinking that instead of bringing up Lily . . . I wish he would've kissed me. How weird is that?

"I told my mom about how you take care of your sister, and she thought you should probably be recommended for sainthood."

"Or committed," I say flippantly. Actually, I'm shocked that Owen told his mother about me. I wonder if he and his mother talk about a lot of things. For some reason I find this concept totally mind-blowing. How is it possible that he would be close to his mom, when my mother usually feels like a stranger to me?

Once again, I get that old feeling like I will never fit in . . . like I'm really an alien dropped down from Planet Weird. Seriously, what do I have in common with this boy who made baklava with his grandma and actually has a relationship with his mother?

10

I repress all alien thoughts, paste a smile on my face, and hold my head high as Owen and I walk up to the multiplex theater. Isn't that what Elizabeth in *Pride and Prejudice* would do?

"Hey, Owen," a male voice calls from behind us. We both turn, and the first person I see is my old "best" friend Katie Wick on the arm of a guy named Miles. I honestly can't remember his last name, but I know he's one of the "elite"—a cool kid. And a friend of Owen's.

"What's up?" Owen asks as he pauses to wait for them to join us. Miles informs Owen that they're going to the same movie, and to my amazement, Katie acts like we're still best friends.

"How are you, Aster? I was just thinking about you today."

I try not to look too shocked. "Really? Why?"

"I was cleaning my room, and I found this cute little pink dragon."

Okay, I know exactly what she means. I won that dragon at the county fair the summer before we went to middle school and she abandoned me for more impressive friends. But I won it, and she wanted it. And, being used to keeping people happy, I gave it to her. I guess I thought it would be some kind of superglue that would bond our friendship. Obviously I was wrong. Still, I do not let a single muscle in my face betray that I remember any of this. "What dragon?"

"Don't you remember?" As we all get into line, she goes on to tell the story, *her* way. She admits that I won it but then says I insisted on giving the dragon to her. If she hadn't given it that little twist, I might've acted like I remembered this, but because of her lie, I play dumb.

"Sorry, I don't really recall that," I say. "Are you sure it was me and not another one of your friends?"

She looks stunned, and I feel ashamed. But there is no going back. Not here. Not now.

"We just had the best dinner at Anatole's," Owen says. I think he senses tension in the air and is trying to change the subject. Bless him!

"Oh, I love Anatole's," Katie gushes. "I'm so envious."

Just then my cell phone rings. I glance at the clock on the front to see that it's 8:52 and nearly time for my mom to come home. Praying that nothing is wrong, I step out of line and answer it.

"Aster," Crystal hisses, "you're going to have to come home."

"Why?"

"Lily is throwing a fit."

I move farther away from the line. "What kind of fit?"

"The kind where she throws things."

"Oh . . . Have you tried to calm her down?"

"Nothing is working."

"Did you put in the second movie? *The Little Mermaid*? She loves that one, and it usually settles her right—"

"It's playing now, and she couldn't care less."

"Well, it's almost nine, and my mom—" I hear a loud crash in the background and am afraid to ask. "What was that?"

"A lamp."

"Oh, dear . . ."

"Come home, Aster, now!"

I glance over to where Owen is just paying for our tickets, and a kind of steely resolve takes hold of me. "No," I say calmly. "My mother will come home."

"When?" she demands.

"Right now," I say. "I'm calling her."

"Fine. I don't care who. Just make it fast."

I force a smile and a tight wave toward Owen, then quickly dial the number for O'Leary's. I wait for my mom to come to the phone, then I say quickly, "Lily is flipping out. I can't get home as quickly as you can, so I told Crystal you'd be there. You better hurry." And I hang up. Not only do I hang up, I turn my phone off! I feel like a criminal as I rejoin Owen, Miles, and Katie. A slightly delirious criminal.

●　　●　　●

Was it worth it? I ask myself as Owen is driving me home. Certainly the movie was not. I don't even remember it. I was sitting there freaking over what might be possibly happening at home. I imagined Lily tying up Crystal and burning the house down, all before my mom got there. Consequently, I asked Owen to take me straight home as soon as we emerged from the theater. And now he's being very quiet.

"I'm sorry," I tell him for the second time. "It's just that I'm worried about Lily."

"But I thought Crystal was—"

"That phone call I got earlier," I admit. "It was from Crystal, and it wasn't going well."

"You should've told me." He turns into my neighborhood. "We could've left—"

"No," I say firmly. "I called my mom. It was time for her to get off work anyway. I told her it was her problem."

Owen nods as if he's impressed. "Good for you."

"Thanks. I've been giving the situation some thought, and I'm coming to the conclusion that it's unfair for me to be solely responsible for Lily."

"I'd have to agree with you. So does my mom."

"So does my sister Rose. I mean, she might be selfish, but I think she's got it right in this case. My mom is taking advantage of me."

"It's because you're so good with Lily," Owen says.

"I know. But it's like I'm being rewarded with more problems because of it."

"It doesn't seem fair."

"Yeah. I think Independence Day is coming for me."

"How does your dad fit into this? I mean, does he take some responsibility for Lily?"

I attempt to explain the situation with my dad. "He tried to stay involved with us girls," I admit. "But it was tricky. My mom was pretty mad at him for leaving."

"That seems only fair."

"Yeah. And it didn't take long for my dad to hook up with someone else. He married Jana about five years ago. At first I thought she was really nice. We used to go over there and visit. But she wasn't really comfortable with Lily . . ."

"So the visits stopped?"

"Also, Jana got pregnant. My dad finally got the son he'd wanted. I have a half brother named Nelson."

"Do you ever see him?"

"I haven't since he was a baby. My parents got into a big fight . . . I'm not even sure what it was about. I mean, besides the same old same old. But after that we didn't go visit anymore. My mom said Dad didn't want us there. She said he had his new family and we didn't fit in." I sigh. "I guess I believed her."

"And your dad doesn't call or anything?"

"No. I mean, he sends birthday and Christmas presents. But that's about it. He doesn't even pay child support."

"Seriously? A guy can go to jail for that."

"Yeah, I'm surprised my mom hasn't gone after him."

Now we're at my house, but I'm not sure I want to go in. All the lights are on, but at least Crystal's car is gone and my mom's is there. I think that's a good sign.

"Are you going to be okay?" Owen asks as he turns off the engine.

I force a smile for his benefit. "Oh yeah, this is probably nothing compared to some of the stuff I've been through."

"I think my mom is right."

"What?"

"You should be given sainthood."

"Don't you have to be dead first?"

"I'm not sure."

Actually, I'm thinking that might be a possibility once I walk in the front door. My mom is going to kill me for this. Okay, not literally. At least, I don't think so.

"Thanks for everything," I tell him. "I'm sorry my life is such a mess. And I don't even blame you if you don't want to see me again."

He just shakes his head. "No problem, Aster. I definitely want to see you again. You are so different than anyone else I know."

"Yeah, you can say that again." I reach for my bag.

"I mean, good different. You are . . . hmm . . . refreshing. Yes. That's the right word. You are refreshing and invigorating." He reaches over and touches my cheek. And suddenly I don't know what to do. I have no response to his strange compliment.

But to my relief, he hops out of the pickup, then dashes around and opens my door before I can. "Thanks," I tell him as he offers his hand. "But you might not want to walk me clear up to the door. My mom could be waiting with a loaded weapon."

"Seriously?" He looks worried.

"Not seriously. But she's going to be really, really ticked at me. There will probably be fireworks coming from our house tonight."

"Okay." He puts his hand on my arm, stopping me while we're still in the shadows of the driveway. He pulls me close to him, and I feel his face next to mine. Then he kisses me. It's a very sweet and gentle kiss, and to my surprise I lean in for more. But he stops it there. "I'll call you tomorrow, okay?"

"Okay," I say breathlessly.

"Take care, Aster." He touches my cheek again, and I feel tingly.

"You too," I call out as he heads back to his pickup. Then I hurry to the house, pull out my key, and let myself in. I quickly close the door behind me, thankful that Owen is safely on his way and unable to hear the yelling match that's going on in here.

"You *will* go to bed!" my mom shouts.

"No! No! No!" Lily screams. Her voice is hoarse and sort of pathetic, like she's been screaming all night and can't hold out much longer.

"Yes, you will!"

"No!"

I hurry to where they're standing in the hallway now. Lily's face is blotchy—red and white—and her eyes are swollen, and despite all my resolve to step aside from the chaos of my life, my heart breaks for her.

"Aster!" she sobs. She comes running to me, throwing her arms around me so forcefully that we both nearly fall over.

I stroke her sweaty hair. "It's okay, Lil," I say into her ear. "Everything's okay." I can feel her melting now. It's as if I'm her savior. And while part of me feels good to be so needed, part of me is sickened by it and wants to vomit.

"It's about time," my mom snaps.

"Go to bed," I tell her. "I'll handle this."

Without saying another word, she stomps off to the other end of the house, and I am left to take a poor, wilted Lily to her bed. Even after I tuck her in, get her a drink, and read her a story, she is still shaking. "You left me," she says in her tired and hoarse voice. "Why you go, Aster?" She's so worn-out that she doesn't even have any anger left. "Why you leave me?"

"I was coming back," I assure her.

"You were gone. Gone, gone. I looked for you. I could not find you. I *need* you, Aster. Don't leave me. *Please.* I *need* you." She sits up and clings to me with fresh, brokenhearted sobs, and suddenly I feel like a piece of baklava, with layer upon layer upon layer of guilt.

11

I can't sleep. Everyone else in the house is home now, sleeping soundly, and I am wide awake. But I can't take lying here in my bed, feigning sleep while the volume inside my head is turned up to high. So I get up and creep out to the living room again. Instead of sitting on the couch and thinking like I usually do, I begin to pace back and forth, as if the movement will bring me an answer . . . or peace. I feel so lost, so alone, so desperate, that I finally just fall on my knees and beg God to help me. Although I've spent what seems like my entire lifetime fixing everything for everyone, it feels like my life is beyond repair.

I stay out there until nearly three in the morning, and then, not really feeling much better, I tiptoe back to bed. When I awake, the sun is shining brightly into my room, and Lily is tapping me on the forehead. "Aster? Aster? Wake up."

I open my eyes and blink into Lily's big pink face about three inches from mine, so close I can smell her breath, which is strong enough to wake the dead. "I'm awake," I grumble, turning to escape her and see the clock. I'm surprised to see that it's nearly ten o'clock. Last night's chaos must've taken its toll on everyone. Fortunately, it's Saturday, so I don't need to get Lily to the rec center today. And *un*fortunately, it's Saturday, so I will have Lily for the entire day and the entire weekend.

"Well, it's about time," Rose says as she comes into the bedroom. She's partially dressed, but her hair is still in hot rollers. "Sounds like you guys had quite a party last night."

Lily, sitting next to my bed like a faithful puppy, just scowls. I lean back into my pillow and close my eyes, wanting to simply disappear.

"Get *up*, Aster," Lily whines. "Time to rise and shine, sunshine!"

This actually makes me smile. This is exactly what I say to her when she sleeps late on a day when she needs to be somewhere. Who knew she was listening.

I open one eye to see her still peering at me. Her brow is creased with concern, and her eyes are sad. "You going to get up, Aster?"

"Yes," I say, mustering false cheer. "See, I'm getting up right now."

"Good."

"You two," Rose says in a tone that suggests disgust, although I think I detect a slight flicker of sympathy in her eyes. Or else I'm just imagining things.

"Okay, Lily, you go make your bed now. See if you can do it the way I showed you, and there will be a prize."

"A prize?" She looks pleased.

"But only if you do it right."

Now she looks puzzled, and I can tell she's trying to recall what I've been attempting to teach her. It's a challenge since we only do it on weekends when we have time.

"Remember the steps," I say intensely, as if I'm telling her how to detonate a bomb. "First you fluff the pillow. Then you smooth the sheets, nice and straight. Then you pull up the bedspread and fold back the edge. Remember?"

She nods. "Yes. I remember."

"Good girl."

Then she leaves as if she's going on mission impossible. And maybe it is. At least it gives me a little break.

"*You* are unbelievable," Rose says. She holds up a hot pink top that I think makes her face look flushed. Of course, I don't say this.

"Meaning?"

"I don't know . . ." Rose just shakes her head. "But I do know this: Mom was really cranky before she left for work this morning. What went on here last night?"

And so, surprising myself, I actually tell Rose what happened. Not everything, but how Crystal called to say Lily was upset and how I called Mom and told her to deal with it. "And then I went to the movie with Owen and some friends, and I turned off my phone."

"No freaking way!" Rose looks truly shocked now.

"Hey, I was in a theater, you're supposed to turn off your phone."

"I mean, no way you told Mom to deal with Lily."

"Way." I stand up, stretch lazily, then hold my head high. "I was on a date, Rose. I was having fun like a normal person. Mom was *supposed* to get off work in like less than five minutes. Do you think I should've come home?"

Rose seems to seriously consider this, then shakes her head. "No. You made the right decision."

I'm floored. "Really?"

"Yeah." She holds up a tangerine-colored top in front of the mirror.

"That one," I say.

"Ya think?"

"Uh-huh, it makes your complexion look pretty."

She smiles. "Okay then."

As she's manipulating the top over her big head of curlers, I decide to take this "sisterly" conversation to the next level. "Rose?"

"Huh?"

"I've been wondering about Dad."

"Dad?" She's got the shirt past the curlers now, pulling it over her bra. "What do you mean?"

"I mean, why did he cut us off like he did? It seemed like he was trying. I know there was Jana and then Nelson came along—Dad's little mini-me—but we still went over there for a while." I glance toward the door and lower my voice. "Was it because of Lily?"

I remember how Jana used to be nervous if Lily was around

the baby without supervision. It's like she thought Lily was going to suffocate him or drop him on his head, when in reality Lily loved the baby.

Rose shrugs. "Lily *and* Mom."

"Huh?"

"It was both of them, Aster. Lily was stressing out Jana."

"Yeah, I know."

"And Mom was stressing out *everyone*."

"What do you mean?" As far as I could recall, my parents never, I mean *never*, talked to each other after Dad left us. If Mom answered the phone and it was him, she would simply hand the phone to Rose or me. Sometimes she even hung up on him.

"I mean, I heard them having a huge argument. We'd been with him for the weekend, and he dropped off you and Lily at the library and brought me home. I'd gone straight to my room, but then I heard shouting, and I realized Dad was still here. I don't think either of them knew I was listening."

"And?"

"And I heard Mom really telling him off, calling him every name in the book. She was so angry. I think if she'd had a gun in her hand, she would've shot him."

"What started the fight?"

"You mean besides Dad leaving?"

"Yeah, I mean that day. What started it?"

Rose frowns. "I didn't hear the beginning. I just heard Mom going nuts. She said she hated him and wished he was dead and rotting in hell. She never wanted to see him again, she wanted him to stay out of our lives. All kinds of nasty stuff."

"Really? You heard all that?"

"Yeah."

"Why didn't you tell me?"

"Why should I?"

Why am I surprised that Rose left me out? Still, it hurts. "So that was it then? He did what she wanted by staying out of our lives?"

"I guess so . . . I mean, we never went back to visit after that. And he stopped calling, and I'm sure it was around then that he stopped paying child support too."

"But that's nuts."

"So what's new?"

I just shake my head, trying to absorb this. My mom tells off my dad. He completely checks out of our lives. And that's supposed to make sense?

"I gotta go to work, Aster." Rose is taking the hot rollers out now, tossing them onto her bed.

"I'm going to call him," I proclaim.

"Dad?" She looks shocked. "You're going to call Dad?"

"Yeah."

"Seriously?"

"Yeah. He's our father, Rose. He should know what our lives are like. And he should be contributing financially. Maybe if he did, we could afford to hire someone to help with Lily."

"Maybe." But she shakes her head. "But whatever you do,

don't tell Mom. I mean, if she was in a bad mood this morning, I cannot imagine how ticked she'd be if you dragged her ex back into the picture. Be careful, Aster."

• • •

After Rose goes to work, I go through the regular Saturday chores and try to get Lily to help, which is frustrating both of us. Then I realize that I actually have no way to go see Dad. And for some reason I feel this is a conversation I need to have face-to-face with him. The phone won't cut it. But I don't have a way to get there, and it's too far to ride my bike, which I couldn't do anyway since there's the Lily factor. The bus doesn't go that far, and even if we rode it to the edge of town and hired a taxi, there's no way I could afford it. I'm tempted to call Crystal, but after last night, she's probably not speaking to me. I suppose I didn't really think this through very well.

It's close to noon now, and Lily has been grumbling about missing story hour at the library. Even though I point out that she's partially to blame since she slept in too, she can't accept it. I'm just beginning to lose patience with her when my cell phone rings, and I'm pleased to see that it's Owen. Great escape. Although I know better than to leave Lily unattended for this conversation. Too risky.

"How's it going?" he asks.

"Okay." Then I briefly describe the chaos I came home to last night, trying not to go into too much detail since Lily is all ears. "But things settled down," I say casually.

"My mom was asking me why you guys don't hire someone to help with Lily."

Man, he really does talk to his mom a lot. "I wish we could afford to do that," I admit.

"She said there are state programs and studies and stuff."

"Yeah, we've looked into some things, but it's hard living in a small town, plus the state always seems to be cutting back the budget."

Now, on one hand it's sweet that Owen cares enough to bring this up, but on the other hand I find it a tiny bit aggravating that his mom thinks she knows more about this sort of thing than we do. I talk to Kellie at the rec center fairly regularly, and she's a real expert on what's available for kids like Lily. Unfortunately, it's not much.

"It's probably none of my business, huh?" Owen says.

"No . . . I mean, it's nice that you care, but there don't seem to be any magic fixes for this sort of thing." *Short of money*, I think, but I don't say this.

"I just think it'd be good for you to get more time for yourself, Aster. It's like you're missing out on, well, you know, all kinds of regular stuff."

"Yeah, I do know." Now I get an idea. "Hey, if you really want to help me, Owen, is there any way you could give Lily and me a ride over to my dad's house today?"

"Where does he live?"

"Renton."

"Really? For some reason I thought he lived far away."

"No, just far enough to make it inconvenient to visit."

"I'd be happy to take you guys. Say when, and I'll be there."

"Well, let me fix Lily some lunch so she won't be grumpy. How about one-ish?"

"One-ish is fine."

I hang up and tell Lily that we're going to Dad's house, and she looks at me like I just told her we're going to the moon.

"Dad's house?"

"Yes. Remember Dad?"

She makes a funny smile. "Yeah. Of course."

"But first you need to eat some lunch."

"Does Dad still have the baby?"

I consider this. "I think so. Except the baby is older now. Let's see . . . Nelson would be about two and a half."

"How big is that?"

I hold my hand down to estimate Nelson's height. "About that tall, I guess. And he can walk and talk now." Okay, that's assuming Nelson is normal.

Suddenly I wonder, what if Nelson is like Lily? Then I re-member that Lily's problem was related to her birth, not ge-netics. I looked up the medical term *umbilical cord prolapse* when I was about ten and discovered that Lily suffered brain damage when her oxygen supply was cut off shortly before she was born. Nelson is probably just fine.

I hurry to get our lunch made and eaten, then take care to make sure Lily looks clean and presentable. I even make her use the fingernail brush, and we cut her nails. Jana was always worried about cleanliness around the baby, like she thought Lily had cooties or something. And besides Jana, I want Dad to look at both of us without being embarrassed to admit we're his children.

I take care with my own appearance too. Of course, I would do this anyway for Owen's sake. I'm not sure what Owen will do while we visit Dad. Hopefully, he won't mind making himself scarce for a while, because there's no way I want him to be around to hear me asking why my father doesn't pay child support. I don't want Owen to hear me demanding money.

● ● ●

As Owen drives Lily and me over to Renton, I am starting to freak. Why on earth did I think I could do this? Should I have called first? Or maybe it's better to just pop in on him without warning. That way he can't skip out on us before we get there. Not that I think he'd do that exactly, but I don't know. Two years is a long time to avoid seeing your daughters.

"This is a nice neighborhood," Owen says after I direct him to the development where Dad lives.

"Yeah. Jana already owned a house here. A pretty nice one too. She's some kind of high-up-there nurse that's almost like a doctor. I think she calls herself a practitioner. Anyway, I guess she makes good money." I can hear my nerves talking now, chattering on and on about things that I'm sure Owen couldn't care less about. But it's like I need to fill the space.

"Jana had never been married before, never had kids, so I

guess she put all her money into the house and things. I heard her say once that she never expected to get married. And she was almost forty when she got pregnant, so that was kind of surprising too." I point to the two-story craftsman-style house. "That's it."

I notice that the house has been repainted a rich olive green with warm brown on the trim. I seriously doubt that this house needed to be repainted since it's still pretty new. Our house, which is not so new, really does need a new paint job.

As Owen pulls into the driveway, three things occur to me almost simultaneously: (1) Dad might not be home; (2) he might not live here anymore, although my last Christmas card with a $100 gift card from Target had this address on it; and (3) he might not even be married to Jana now, although that seems unlikely.

"Do you want me to stick around?" Owen asks. I can tell he's uneasy.

"Well, maybe just until I make sure everything is okay," I say nervously. "I mean, I didn't even think that he might not be home."

"Why don't you go and check. I'll wait here."

"Okay." Still, it feels like my rear is glued to the upholstery. I'm not sure I really want to do this. I'm not sure I *can* do this. Suddenly this seems like one of the nuttiest things I've ever done.

"There's Dad!" Lily shouts, pointing over to the side of the house where a man is pulling a hose. How she knew it was Dad beats me, because he has a full beard, and I'm not even sure I would've recognized him. Although the red hair is kind of a giveaway.

"Okay then." I glance at Owen, and he gives me an encouraging smile.

"Good luck," he says.

"Thanks."

"Come on, Aster," Lily urges. She's opening the passenger door now, halfway out. And the bearded man is looking curiously at the strange white pickup parked in his driveway.

"I'll have my cell phone on," Owen says. "I'll probably go grab a bite to eat and check out that new electronics store."

"Great," I say, although I'm not really listening. It's like my ears are buzzing with nerves and my hearing is impaired. I watch Lily streaking across the driveway straight for Dad, like she thinks he's going to give her a big hug, and I'm thinking he probably doesn't recognize this bulky teenage girl.

"I better go," I tell Owen, quickly jumping down from the truck. Then I follow Lily, forcing a weak smile. I send a cautious little wave to my father. "Hey, Dad, what's up?"

12

"What's going on, Aster?" My dad's expression is a cross between surprise and irritation.

"We just thought we'd stop by and say hi," I tell him.

"Yeah," Lily says. "Hi, Dad. Where you been?"

"I've been right here." He's smiling at Lily, but there's a stiffness in his face.

"Sorry to catch you by surprise," I say. "I guess I should've called."

He nods and then seems to relax ever so slightly. "Yeah, calling would be good. Still, it's great to see you two. Where's Rosie?"

"Not Rosie!" Lily says with authority. "Just Rose."

"Yeah, she throws a fit if anyone calls her Rosie, Dad."

"Good to know," he says.

"Anyway, she's at work. She's still working at Delilah's."

"Man, you girls have grown." He sighs loudly, then eyes Lily like he wants to ask how she got so fat, but thankfully, he doesn't say anything. Then he stares at me. "Wow, Aster, you got tall. How tall are you anyway?"

"About five ten."

"Just a couple inches shorter than your old man."

"Daddy!" a child's voice yells from around the side of the house.

"Oh, I almost forgot about Nelson." He dashes back and returns with a blond toddler in his arms. He reintroduces us, and Lily gets down on her knees in an attempt to hug him, but Nelson backs away like he's not too sure about this big girl.

"Don't scare him, Lily," I warn her. "Little kids take time to get to know people."

"Hi, Nelson," she says in a babyish voice. "Wanna play with Lily?"

He nods but keeps his distance.

"Let's go in the backyard," Dad says. He herds us back along the side of the house and through a gate. I wonder if he's afraid to let us in the house. Maybe Jana will throw a fit or throw us out. But then I see that he seems to be working on putting together a play structure.

"That looks fun," Lily says as she grabs hold of a swing.

"Not yet, Lily," Dad warns. "I have to sturdy some things up before it can be used."

But then Nelson gets on the swing and Dad doesn't say anything, which makes me think he was worried that the structure wasn't strong enough to bear Lily's weight. But Lily seems oblivious to this as she starts to push Nelson in the swing. Dad stands nearby like he's worried she'll push him too high or cause him to fall out. But Lily is actually being very careful.

"Hey, Aster, why don't you give me a hand with this," he says as he picks up a yellow plastic slide that's lying on the grass.

So I end up helping my dad put together a play structure for my half brother while Lily keeps him occupied by swinging then playing kickball. They end up in the sandbox, where Lily seems to be having the time of her life.

"Lily is good with Nelson," I point out.

"So far, so good."

"Meaning you don't trust her?"

"She's got the mentality of a preschooler, Aster. You don't let a preschooler babysit a toddler."

"It's not like she's alone with him. I'm just saying that Nelson seems to like her. And she certainly likes him. I think it's sweet."

Now Dad smiles at me, and it seems like the first genuine smile he's had since we arrived. "Yeah, you're right. It is sweet." Now he just stares at me again, slowly shaking his head like he's trying to figure things out. "You've sure grown up, Aster."

"I'll be seventeen next week," I remind him.

Dad gets ready to put together what looks like the final part on this structure. "Darn, I'm missing a bolt."

I go over and peruse the pile of junk that must've come in the kit—various screws and washers and stuff—but I can't find this elusive bolt either.

Then Dad's eyes light up. "Hey, maybe you and Lil could keep an eye on Nelson while I make a quick run to the hardware store to get another one. It'll be so much easier than loading him into his car seat and—"

"Sure," I tell him. "Go ahead. And don't worry, I'll keep a close eye on Nelson and Lily."

I assume this means Jana isn't in the house today, and that is a huge relief. I can talk freely to Dad without Jana popping in and putting in her two cents. Not that I dislike her that much, but I guess I don't really trust her, and I'm pretty sure she doesn't like Lily or me. She and Rose seemed to get along okay at first, but that sort of cooled off after the baby came. Especially when Rose informed Jana that she "didn't care to babysit Nelson." Big surprise there, since Rose never helped much with Lily either. And, naturally, I wasn't any help to Jana, being that I was—still am—sort of joined at the hip to Lily. My guess is Jana hasn't missed the Flynn girls much.

So I go sit on the edge of the sandbox and watch as Nelson and Lily play. They really do seem to get along nicely, and I think for the next several years they could probably be friends. Until Nelson outgrows her or begins to feel embarrassed to be around her. I'm sure it will happen.

● ● ●

Dad returns with the bolt after about twenty minutes. By then Nelson is starting to get a little cranky, and Dad announces it's naptime.

"For me too?" Lily asks. Sometimes I make her take a nap.

"Not you," I say.

"Uh, do you girls want to come inside?" Dad offers in a way that suggests he's not quite comfortable with the concept. I suspect this has to do with his neat-freak wife.

"Yes!" Lily says. "I'm thirsty."

So we follow Dad and Nelson through the French doors that go into the family room. Their family room is about twice as big as ours, and everything matches. I mean really matches, like Jana picked it all out at the same time or maybe even from a catalog. Rose thinks it's beautiful, but I think it feels phony. Lily just likes the big-screen TV.

"Aster, why don't you get Lily and yourself something to drink," Dad says. "I'll get Nelson off to dreamland."

"Dreamland," Lily says in a wistful voice.

Lily decides she wants Pepsi, and I settle for water. We both just stand in the kitchen, because I don't want Lily to spill her soda on the cream-colored rug in the family room. Dad comes back, gets himself a beer, and asks us if we want to sit down.

"Maybe at the breakfast bar," I suggest, nodding to Lily and her soda.

Dad seems to get this. So we all three sit at the breakfast bar, and Lily does spill some Pepsi when she spins around too fast on the bar stool. I give her a warning as I run for some paper towels. Then I sop up her spill, wipe her face, and tell her to drink the last sip, which she does. I take the can over to the sink, rinse it out, and turn to see Dad staring at me again.

"Where does this go?" I ask.

"Just leave it in the sink, I'll get it later."

So I set the can and my glass in the sink, then turn to face my dad, who is still sitting at the breakfast bar between us. Lily has wandered into the family room, where she has discovered a basket of picture books and seems content.

"I'm sure you're wondering about this surprise visit," I say quietly. "And I don't want to play games, so I'm just going to come right out with it."

He nods. "Okay."

"Why haven't you been paying child support for the past two years?"

Dad frowns, then runs his fingers through his beard. "Didn't your mom tell you that I'm not working?"

"You're not working?" This stuns me. How can Dad, the guy who used to be a total workaholic, not be working?

"No, I quit when Nelson was really small. You see, Jana decided—I mean, *we* decided that one of us needs to stay home with Nelson until he starts kindergarten. He was getting sick so much from the day-care center that we were worried about his health, and Jana was missing work when she had to go get him all the time." Dad holds up his hands. "Anyway, since Jana makes more money than I do and she had the best health insurance and benefits, I was nominated to be the main caregiver for our son."

"So you're a stay-at-home dad?"

"Just call me Mr. Mom."

"Seriously?"

"Yep. And let me tell you, it gets old fast."

I glance over at Lily. "You don't have to tell *me*."

"Yeah, I guess not."

"Even so, Dad, aren't you still *supposed* to pay child support? I mean, isn't it a law?"

"When I told your mom about this development a couple years ago, I explained that since my income was going to be reduced to zero, it would be impossible to pay child support, and as you can imagine that didn't go over too well."

"So I heard." I don't point out that I just learned of this recently.

"Anyway, your mom pretty much told me that if I didn't pay child support, I wouldn't be allowed to see you girls at all—ever."

I blink. "She really said that?"

"Yep."

"So that's why we haven't seen you."

"She explicitly told me that if I had any more to do with you girls other than sending you things for birthdays and holidays, she would talk to a lawyer."

"Oh yeah . . . now it's beginning to make sense."

"Didn't she tell you any of this?" Dad asks.

"No. If the subject of you comes up, which it seldom does, Mom gets angry, and that's pretty much the end of it."

"Well, your mother also said that as soon as I start working again, she will go after the five years of unpaid child support, which means I won't be bringing much of a salary home. I, uh, I haven't told Jana this yet."

And I assume that Jana hasn't offered to help Dad pay child support for the three girls she can barely tolerate. In fact, I suspect that Jana is perfectly happy with this little arrangement. Dad gets to stay home and take care of their child, plus they don't get stuck with child support. Nice setup.

"So I don't really know what I can do for you, Aster." He holds his hands up again in that helpless gesture. "Unless I go back to work, which sounds tempting, although Jana would throw a fit."

"You wouldn't want that to happen."

He forces a weak-looking smile. "No . . . I wouldn't."

"So is it all you hoped it would be, Dad, to have a son?" I hear the bitterness in my voice, and as much as I don't like it, I don't think I can help it. I am angry. Really angry.

"Well, I have to admit that for as much work as that little bugger makes for me, he's a lot of fun too."

"Yeah, sometimes I feel like that about Lily." I narrow my eyes at my dad and lower my voice. "But I don't get off caring for her for *only five years*. It's been more like most of my life. Not that I have a life, really. It's hard to when you have a full-time job taking care of a—" I stop myself from saying "retard." I know that's wrong. And it's not really how I feel. But I am frustrated. More at Dad than Lily.

Just then we hear the door to the garage opening, and I turn to see Jana coming in. She looks as shocked to see me as

I am to see her. She has on some kind of medical garb, kind of a like a doctor, I suppose.

"Why, Aster," she says with raised brows, "what are you doing here? Is anything wrong?"

"Yeah," I say flippantly. "Something is wrong. But I don't see that it's ever going to be made right."

This only makes her look more confused, so Dad gives her a quick explanation, leaving a few things out.

"Does your mother know you're here?" Jana asks.

"No. And she won't find out about it either. Otherwise she might try to charge Dad for seeing us. Not that he'd pay." I walk into the family room, where Lily is immersed in a Care Bears pop-up book.

"Come on, Lily." I reach for the book, close it, and place it in the basket. "It's time to go home."

"But I wanna look at the—"

"We'll go look at books at the library." I grab her hand and pull her to her feet. "At least those books are free. We can afford that." As she stands, she notices Jana, and I think she gets that maybe we aren't wanted here. Lily's eyes grow wide as I pull her past Dad and his wife. I lead her through the house and out the front door, then slam it behind us.

"Are you mad, Aster?" We're out on the sidewalk now, and as I dial Owen's cell phone number, Lily studies me with a confused frown.

"Actually, I am a little mad."

"At that girl?" Lily calls all females girls.

"Yes. Do you remember Jana?"

"Yeah. She mean."

"Yes," I agree. "She is." I want to add that Dad is mean too, but I don't want to poison Lily. In fact, I am beginning to get an idea . . . an idea that could buy me some free time.

Lily and I walk several blocks. I can't bear to just stand out there in the front yard like Dad's reject kids, the ones he threw away so he could start a new life.

"How'd it go?" Owen asks when he finally meets up with us down the street.

I force a smile. "How about if I fill you in on it later."

"Oh yeah." He nods toward Lily. "I get you."

"I played with Nelson," Lily announces. Then she tells Owen about the sandbox and the swing and the basket of pretty books.

"Sounds like you had fun, Lily," Owen says.

"I did." Then she looks cautiously at me. "I think I did. Did I, Aster?"

This makes me laugh. "Yes, Lily, you did have fun. Then Jana came home, and it was time to go."

"Because Jana is mean."

As Owen drives us home, Lily babbles on about how she spilled Pepsi and the pop-up dragon book and lots of Lily-like things. But I'm being quiet because I'm making a plan—an independence plan. I think it could work too. But only if I can get my mom to agree. That will be the big challenge. And I realize this might require some research on my part. I

133

might need to find out about visitation rights and perhaps a bit more about child support laws. I might even become an expert on family law.

● ● ●

"Thanks for the ride," I tell Owen when we get home.

"I hope it helped."

"We'll see," I say.

"Do you want to do anything later tonight?"

I'm about to say no when I realize that a night out might be just the ticket to kick this thing off, not to mention it will get my mother's attention.

I wait until Lily is out of the pickup to answer. "I'd love to do something tonight. And my mom doesn't work late on Saturdays, so she can spend the evening with Lily."

Owen's eyes light up. "Cool."

I nod. "Yeah, way cool."

"What time does your mom get home?"

"Around six."

"Should I pick you up then?"

I grin at him. "Yep. That'd be perfect."

Of course, as I unlock the door I realize this could present another problem. Being that it's Saturday, I usually go to youth group with Crystal, and we always take Lily with us. However, based on how things went with Lily and Crystal just last night, I wouldn't be surprised if we don't hear from Crystal today. And I know that I won't be calling her. If Lily asks, I'll just have to explain that that's what comes of being naughty like she was last night. Because, as Kellie always points out, consequences can be the best lessons for kids like Lily. Unfortunately, special needs kids often need the same consequences over and over, and that can be exhausting for some of us. But I'll be out of that picture tonight.

13

"You're doing what?" Mom demands as we face off in the kitchen. I've just told her my plans for the evening.

"I'm going out tonight," I repeat calmly. "I have a date with Owen. He'll be here soon."

"What about youth group . . . and Lily?"

I make a skeptical face. "Really, Mom, did you think that Crystal would drive us there after the way Lily treated her last night?"

"*I'll* drive you," Mom says quickly.

"Oh?" I feign surprise. "I didn't even think of that."

"Well, I will—"

"Sorry, Mom, it's too late. I already made plans, and I'm sure Owen is on his way over here right now."

"Why don't you and Owen take Lily to youth group then?" I hear a slight note of pleading in her voice now. She so does not want to be stuck at home alone with Lily tonight. Well, join the club.

"Owen doesn't go to that youth group."

"What if I drop Lily at youth group?" Poor Mom. She is desperate.

But this actually makes me laugh. I put a hand on Mom's shoulder. "No way, Mom. You don't get it, but Lily couldn't possibly handle being at youth group on her own. Of course, if you were to stay there with her, it might—"

"No." Mom shakes her head firmly.

Now Lily joins us in the kitchen and is looking at me with suspicion. I'm sure she notices that I have changed clothes and I have my purse. "Where we going?" she asks.

"I am going out with Owen tonight," I say calmly. Really, I don't want to rock her boat. Just then I hear the doorbell and feel like shouting hallelujah, but I don't. "And you get to stay home with Mom."

"No!" Lily shouts.

I just lean over and kiss her cheek. "Yes," I say firmly. "And you be a good girl, okay?"

"No!" she shouts even louder. "No! No! No!" She even attempts to block my way, but I'm prepared for this and take a different route. Poor Lily. She is still screaming "No! No! No!" as I bolt out the door. And yes, I do feel guilty.

"Everything okay in there?" Owen asks with a worried look.

"I have no idea." I take out my phone and turn it off as he walks me to the pickup. "But I think we should hurry and get out of here."

As Owen drives, I explain about part one of my independence plan, involving my parents in the care and maintenance of Lily Flynn. "My mom needs a taste of what my life is really like," I tell him. "That way she'll take me seriously when I suggest that she should allow visitation again, so that Dad can enjoy his fair share of Lily time too."

"You are so smart." Owen chuckles. "Wicked smart."

I laugh. "I just hope that Lily survives."

"She seems like a survivor to me."

And that's exactly what I tell myself every time I think of her this evening. Because Lily is a survivor. She's probably tougher than all of us. And yet I know she has a tender heart as well. I hate to hurt her. And so I pray for her. But that just makes me feel guilty because not only did I ditch Lily tonight, I ditched youth group too.

● ● ●

"You're being pretty quiet," Owen observes as we're finishing dinner. Tonight it's just the Burger Joint, but I appreciate it all the same. And I guess I can't expect fine Greek food every night.

"Sorry."

"You're worried about Lily, aren't you?"

I blink. "Yeah, how'd you guess?"

"Let's just say that you'll probably never be a good poker player."

"Why not? I'm actually pretty good with cards."

"Maybe. But you wouldn't be good at bluffing. No poker face."

"Oh, that's because I wasn't trying. Trust me, when I need to bluff I have no problems with it."

He nods. "Somehow I believe you."

"Got any cards?"

He laughs. "I have a better idea."

"What?"

"It's Miles Atwood's birthday party tonight. I wasn't really planning on going, but it might be fun. You want to go?"

I know enough about Miles Atwood to know that if it's his party, it probably involves booze. And I'm not really into that. Okay, I'm not into that at all. At least I never have been before. "I don't know . . ."

"Miles is an old friend, Aster. And I feel kind of guilty for blowing him off on his birthday."

"I know . . . but I'm not sure I'd fit in."

"Sure you'd fit in." He grins at me. "You'd be the prettiest girl there."

I consider this. Does he really think I'm talking about looks? Or maybe he's just saying what he thinks I want to hear.

"That's not it, Owen. I'm just not comfortable with that whole scene."

"How do you know?"

"I just know. And I don't really drink, Owen. I mean alcohol. And I know that these parties—"

"Let's make a deal," he says suddenly.

"What?"

"We'll go to the party, and if you're not comfortable there, we can just leave. Okay?"

"Really?"

He runs his hand through my hair and smiles. "Do you think I'd make you stick around if you didn't like it, Aster?"

"No . . . I don't think you would."

"Anyway, we'll just pop in and say happy birthday, and if you don't like how it feels, we can just leave. Deal?"

"Deal." Really, I tell myself, how bad could that be? "So where is the party anyway?"

"Katie Wick's house."

For some reason I find this comforting. I've been to Katie's house lots of times, back when we were "best" friends, and I can't imagine her parents allowing her to have a drinking party.

"Sounds great," I say.

●　●　●

It's about 7:30 when we get there, and Katie's big circular driveway looks like a used car lot. Owen parks on the street, and we casually stroll up to the open front door and go inside. Balloons and streamers are everywhere, the music is loud, and the house is packed with guests.

We press our way through the crowd, and I can feel people looking at me, probably wondering what I'm doing here, or what I'm doing with Owen. I just try to act cool. Poker face.

We finally make it to the family room, which has been

cleared of furniture to create a dance floor, and I notice that Katie now has a big inground pool in the backyard.

"Owen," Katie says as she comes over to join us. She has on a pale yellow sundress that shows off her golden tan. Suddenly I feel underdressed in my khaki shorts, Gap T-shirt, and flip-flops. "And Aster too!" She smiles as if she means it, and I begin to relax a bit. "I'm so glad you guys came. The party boy is out by the pool. We're just getting ready to do the cake. Help yourself to drinks and whatever."

"Thanks, Katie," I say. "Cool pool."

She nods. "Dad put that in a couple years ago. There's a hot tub too. Did you bring a suit?"

I shake my head. "No. I didn't realize we were coming here tonight."

"Well, I'm glad you did."

And somehow I believe her.

"Let's go say hi to Miles," Owen says.

"And get some fresh air," I add. Sometimes I can begin to feel claustrophobic in a crowded room or even an elevator. I begin to imagine there's not enough oxygen for everyone.

Out on the patio, I notice that Owen grabs what appears to be a beer from the cooler. Now, I'm determined not to make a big deal about one single beer, but I am wondering how I'll feel if he drinks more than that. Will I want him to drive? Will I ask for his keys? What will I do? Was it a mistake to come here?

"They've got sodas in the cooler too," he tells me as he

pops open the can. So I fish through the ice, digging past what's mostly beer, until I locate a Squirt. Then I go and join Owen and Miles on the other side of the pool. They're both on chaises, and since there's not another place to sit, Owen pats the front part of his chaise. "There's room for two here."

I sit down in front of him, and to my surprise he pulls me back to lean against him. I don't know why, but it makes me uncomfortable. I mean, sure, we've kissed, and I really do like him, but leaning against a guy like this, in front of God and everyone, and at a drinking party . . . well, it just feels awkward. And yet, to be honest, it feels kind of good too. So I stay leaning against him, pop open my soda, and listen as he and Miles talk about baseball. And, as shallow as it sounds, I begin to feel like I'm as cool as everyone else here. Or nearly.

And it's a relief not to have to carry on a conversation. For one thing, I'm kind of in shock that I'm here at all. But besides that, it gives me a chance to observe others. While Owen and Miles talk sports, I people watch. And this is what I see: teenagers trying to act like adults. Or how they think adults act. But mostly they look ridiculous, and I wonder why they don't want to do something that's more fun than drinking, smoking, flirting, and making out. Why are those activities considered to be fun?

Then Katie comes out with a big sheet cake. Like the rest of the decorations, it's our school colors (black and gold), but I must say that black frosting has no appeal to me, and I wonder what everyone's teeth will look like after a few bites.

Before long they all gather around Miles. And since I'm sitting right next to him, with Owen, I suddenly feel like I'm in the limelight too, and I'm not sure I like it. We all sing "Happy Birthday," and Miles blows on the eighteen candles, but they're those candles that refuse to go out. I got them for Lily's twelfth birthday, and she blew and blew and finally got mad when she realized the joke. She was afraid her wish wouldn't come true. But Miles just laughs at his still-burning candles. No big deal . . . he's probably used to having all his dreams come true. Then Katie leans down to kiss him on the mouth. She lingers for what seems a long time, and she's bent over so low that her top gaps and her cleavage is like in-your-face. And I notice that Owen is looking too.

"Happy birthday, baby," she tells Miles in a very seductive voice.

Now I don't even know why, but this whole scene just triggers something inside of me. And suddenly I feel mad. Really, really mad. I mean, *where are Katie's parents?* How do they feel about her throwing a party with alcohol? What do they think about all these kids who are having way more than just one beer and will eventually drive home? Aren't there laws that hold people responsible for serving booze to minors and drivers?

If anyone here could read my mind, they would probably laugh and call me a party pooper, or worse. But I think that out of all these kids pretending to be adults, I am probably the most grown-up person here.

Katie carries the birthday cake back into the house. I stand up and tell Owen that I'm going to get him a piece of cake, but I actually plan to give Katie a piece of my mind. I find her in the kitchen studying the sheet cake with a big knife.

"Need any help?" I offer, thinking this might be a good way to win her trust so she'll listen to me.

"Sure. Want to cut this into about fifty squares and put it onto plates?"

"Sounds like a plan."

"So you and Owen seem fairly serious," she says as we work together.

I shrug. "We only started going out this week."

"Well, I think he really likes you." She tosses me an uncomfortable glance as she plops a scoop of ice cream onto a black paper plate, then hands it to me for cake. "Uh, has he met Lily?"

"Yeah. He's not only met her, he's chauffeured us around town. Lily likes him." Oh, she's probably not thinking very fond thoughts toward him tonight . . . or me either, for that matter, but I don't tell Katie this.

"That's nice. Owen really is a good guy."

"Yeah."

Now a couple other girls come in and offer to help. Katie gives them trays to load the cake pieces on and deliver them. Then it's just Katie and me again. "So . . ." I begin carefully. "I assume your parents aren't home tonight."

She laughs. "No way. They went to the beach for the week-end."

"But they're okay with you having this party?"

"Oh, sure. They really like Miles. I think my mom is hoping we'll get married someday . . . I mean, after college, of course."

"Of course." I slide another piece of cake onto a paper plate, then wipe the frosting off the knife onto a golden napkin. It makes a smear that resembles black tar—oh so appetizing. "So, are your parents okay with the alcohol here?"

"Are you kidding?" She rolls her eyes. "You do remember my parents, don't you? Total teetotalers."

"That's kinda what I thought. So I was a little surprised there was booze here, Katie. Aren't you worried?"

"Worried?" She turns and looks at me with those big "innocent" blue eyes. "About what? My parents won't be home until Tuesday, and that's plenty of time to clean everything up. Miles even offered to pay for a cleaning service, and I stashed all the breakables away. It's under control."

"But what about kids who drink here and then drive home?"

She frowns slightly, then shrugs. "That's not really my problem."

"I don't know . . . I mean, I've heard that the person supplying alcohol can be held accountable if there's a drunk driving incident."

"Oh, well, that would be Miles's problem then. He supplied all the booze."

"Yeah, right." I can see I'm beating a dead horse here.

"I thought you were cool, Aster. But you're starting to sound like a wet blanket." Then she opens the fridge and pulls out what looks like some kind of fruity alcoholic beverage. She opens it and takes a swig, as in, "So there!"

"Excuse me for caring," I say in an aggravated voice.

She takes another swig. "You know, Aster, you are a real buzzkill."

I nod, set down the knife, and walk out of the kitchen. She's right. I am a buzzkill. And I know what I need to do now. I need to get out of here. This is nuts. But when I find Owen, he's just popped open another beer.

"Hey, where's my cake?" he asks me.

"I, uh, I forgot. And I'd like to go now."

He frowns with disappointment. "But the party's barely begun, Aster."

Now I fold my arms across my front and look down at him. Has he forgotten his promise that we could leave if I was uncomfortable? "I'm not really comfortable here," I say quietly.

He seems to consider this. "Just relax, Aster. Have a piece of cake. Chill. We'll go pretty soon, okay?"

I notice now that there are several empty beer cans between him and Miles. I want to ask him if that's his second beer, or has he had more? Then I realize that if I *have* to ask, I should probably just get out of here and find another way home. So, without saying anything, I just nod and then casually stroll back into the house like it's no big deal.

Owen probably assumes I'm helping Katie in the kitchen or getting something to eat or whatever. Or maybe he doesn't care. Maybe, like Katie, he thinks I'm a real buzzkill. Maybe he would be relieved to get rid of me.

Seriously, why did I ever think this would work? What made me think I could fit in—or that I'd even want to fit in—with this crowd? I guess I really am a misfit. But maybe I don't care. Maybe it's better to be yourself and an outsider than to lose your soul just to fit in.

Even so, I'm disappointed in Owen, and I feel a huge lump growing in my throat as I walk through the house toward the front door. But no way do I want anyone here to see me crying. I hold my head high as I push my way through the noisy partyers. It's obvious that some kids are already getting wasted, and it smells pretty bad in the house, although I suspect it'll smell worse before the night ends. A girl who looks like she's about to barf seems to confirm this. With a hand over her mouth, she's staggering down the hallway. I hope she makes it to the bathroom in time, but then again I don't think I care. It's Katie's problem, not mine. God knows I have enough problems of my own to deal with.

Finally I make it out to the front yard, and I just stand there and wonder, *What next?* I'm sure anyone else in my position—a teen trying to be responsible and avoid a potentially bad situation—would call a parent to pick her up. That's probably the normal thing to do. But if I call my mom, who is probably still angry at me and still dealing with Lily, I will only incur her wrath, and I seriously doubt she'd offer to pick me up. She'd probably tell me to walk, and it's like four miles home.

If I call my dad, he'll probably make up some lame excuse like "Jana won't let me use the car tonight" or "I can't afford gas" or "I have to take care of my sweet little boy." I even consider Crystal, although that seems doubtful after last night. Besides, she's probably still at youth group.

Youth group at the church!

Suddenly I realize that our church isn't all that far from here, less than a mile even. In fact, it was Katie who first introduced me to that church, back when she used to go regularly. Of course, you don't see her there anymore, unless it's Christmas or Easter, although her parents still go. Anyway, if I hurry I can make it in time to possibly snag a ride with Crystal. I mean, what can she do? Refuse to give a friend in need a ride? Right there in front of the youth pastor? (She has a secret crush on Pastor Geoff and always acts more "spiritual" when he's watching.)

Blinking back tears, I hurry down the street. Once I'm out of sight of Katie's house, like I think anyone is watching, I begin to run. It's not easy to run in flip-flops, but it's a good distraction to this painful ache that's growing inside of me. This realization that Owen isn't really who I thought he was. Not really.

I should probably be relieved that I figured it out when I did—that I got away before he really broke my heart. Although I'm afraid it's still too late. It hurts. It hurts like someone plunged that big knife I used to cut the cake straight into my stomach and then twisted it a few times.

14

I'm out of breath and my chest is aching when I finally make
it to the church parking lot. But Crystal's car isn't there. In
fact, there are only a couple of cars parked back by the youth
house. The beat-up minivan belongs to Pastor Geoff, and I'm
not sure about the other old clunker. But I am sure of this—I'm
not going to ask Pastor Geoff for a ride tonight. It's not that
I don't like him. He's nice for an older dude. But I know he'll
want to know why I'm here this late, why I wasn't at youth
group, why I'm out of breath, and, perhaps worst of all, why
I'm crying. I realize that my face is wet not with sweat but
with tears. Anyway, as miserable as I feel right now, it would
only make it much, much worse to have to admit how stupid
I've been.

I lean against a lamppost that's not turned on, or maybe it's
burned-out like me. I attempt to catch my breath and stop this
stupid crying. But it's doing no good. Finally I just collapse
down into a squatting position, wrap my hands around my
knees, bow my head, and cry.

"Aster?" I hear a deep voice say my name, and for a moment I think maybe it's God. But I look up to see a vaguely familiar face. It's a guy who recently moved to town and has been coming to youth group. He's kind of tall and gawky and never says much, and I can't even remember his name, but he seems to have remembered mine.

"Yeah?" I say without getting up. I wipe my cheeks and wish the parking lot would open up and swallow me.

"Are you all right?" He has a slightly British-sounding accent.

"Does it look like I'm all right?" I spit out at him.

He shakes his head and offers me a hand. Reluctantly I take it, and slowly he pulls me to my feet. "You actually look a bit like a train wreck," he says.

"I feel like a train wreck."

"Are you on your own?"

"Does it look like anyone is with me?" I don't know why I'm being so rude, but it doesn't seem to faze him.

"No . . . but why are you out here? I don't recall seeing you at youth group."

"That's because I wasn't at youth group." I look him in the eyes, realizing he's about six inches taller than me. "I was at a drinking party." I wait for his reaction.

"Did you have a good time?"

"Does it look like I had a good time?"

"Not so much."

Pastor Geoff comes out, notices us, and begins to approach. "Hey, George," he calls out. "Is something wrong?"

150

"No," George—so that's his name—calls back. "We're all right, thanks."

"Is that Aster with you?"

"Yeah. I'm just giving her a lift. No worries, mate."

"Okay then. Missed you and Lily tonight, Aster. Hope everything's okay."

"Everything is just peachy, thanks!" I say.

He sort of chuckles, then gets into his van and drives away.

"So then, am I giving you a lift home?" He nods toward a tanklike vehicle, some old gas hog from the seventies.

"I'd appreciate that. Sorry I'm being so mean."

"Sounds like you've had a rough go."

So then, for no particular reason, I dump the entire story on him about going to the party with my supposed boyfriend and saying what I did to the hostess and how she called me a buzzkill.

"Buzzkill?" he asks. We're sitting in his car now, but he hasn't turned on the engine yet.

"Like a killjoy, spoilsport, party pooper. Where are you from anyway, George? Australia?"

"Close. New Zealand. But I've lived in the States for a few years. Just can't seem to shake the accent."

"It's actually rather charming," I admit.

He laughs. "Well, you could've fooled me. I reckoned you were about to belt me out there in the parking lot."

"I guess I did want to hit something. Sorry about that."

"No worries."

"Anyway, that's why I ended up here with no ride. The guy I was with was drinking, and I started worrying about him driving, and everything just felt all wrong."

"So that's why you're so upset?"

"I guess that's not the whole reason." I sigh loudly. "But the rest of my story is kind of long . . ."

"How about we get a soda or something? Then you can tell me the whole story, if you like. Unless it's too late."

"No, it's not too late." My guess is that Mom hasn't gotten Lily to bed yet. And, even though tonight's been a disaster, I'm still not ready to let go of my freedom fight.

"Do you like A&W?"

"Are you kidding? I love root beer."

"All right, root beer it is."

●　●　●

Soon we are sitting in the drive-in section of A&Dubs, and I am not only having root beer, I'm having a root beer float. This was George's suggestion, and in my opinion, a good one. What better way to drown one's sorrows than in root beer and ice cream?

By the time we finish, I've told him everything—about Lily and my mom and dad and even Rose.

"So, George," I say as I pass him my empty mug, "what would Jesus do?"

He seems to consider this. "Well . . . I do recall that Jesus told us to love our neighbors as we love ourselves, right?"

"Yeah."

"And it seems you've put a lot of energy into loving Lily, and even the rest of your family, by the way you care for her. But I reckon I'd question how well you've been loving yourself."

I think about this. "I guess I thought that by going out with Owen . . . well, that was kind of like loving myself. I mean, I was doing something that I wanted to do. And before that stupid party, Owen made me feel good and even loved."

"But you weren't feeling too good or too loved tonight."

"No."

He places both our mugs on the tray hooked over his window. "I don't claim to have answers, but it seems to me that you were a bit out of your element at that drinking party, right?"

"Absolutely. I still can't believe Owen was so callous. I mean, he had promised me that we'd leave if I was uncomfortable, but then he started drinking, and it's like he didn't even care. He probably hasn't even noticed I'm gone."

"Alcohol changes people."

"I know." I turn in my seat to see him better.

"My dad has a serious drinking problem. That's the main reason my mom and I moved to the States. She was originally from here but hadn't been back in ages. Anyway, one night after a particularly bad rampage, my mom laid down the law. She told him she'd leave if he didn't quit."

"And?"

"And . . . he made his choice, and we made ours. We left."

"Sad."

"Yeah. But also a relief to get away. He was an ugly drunk."

"I don't think Owen is an ugly drunk," I say. "But thoughtless."

"My mom says that alcohol brings out the true nature of a person. I'm not trying to knock this Owen bloke, but maybe he was pretending to be nice, yet underneath it all, he's a bit selfish."

I consider this. "Maybe."

"Anyway, I think it was rude of him to break his promise to you."

I nod. "Yeah. I do too." Then I smile at George. "But it did allow me to get to know you a little better. I thought you were really shy."

"It's just the way I am in new situations. I like to listen and observe people before I get too involved. Like you and your sister . . . I've been watching you two."

"Really?"

"Yeah. I have to admit I'm impressed with the way you are with Lily. It shows a lot of maturity. I really respect that."

"Wow . . . thanks."

"In fact, seeing you and Lily convicted me of something."

"Convicted you? What do you mean?"

"I mean, God used you to remind me of a bloke back in New Zealand that I hadn't been very nice to."

"I can't imagine you not being nice."

He laughs. "You thought the same thing about Owen too. Remember?"

"I guess. But what happened with that other, what did you call him—bloke?"

"Yeah. A bloke. He was on the soccer team, but really lousy. He had absolutely no skills, but he was the coach's nephew. I was captain of the team, and we were pretty good, and I couldn't see why the coach even played this bloke. What I didn't realize was that Jamie was . . . well, you know, mentally challenged. Oh, he could read and write a bit, but he wasn't in a normal school. Anyway, one time he blew it bad, and I called him some names, like 'stupid,' 'idiot,' 'retard' . . . I can't even remember. We all did it. But it totally crushed him. He ran off and quit the team. I felt bad about it then, but seeing how patient you are with Lily . . . well, I went home and wrote a letter to Jamie and sent it via the coach, apologizing for my meanness." George shrugs. "I don't know if it made him feel any better, but I know I needed to do it."

"Good for you."

He sighs sadly. "It's hard to undo 'stupid.'"

"And now you're making me feel guilty," I say.

"Why's that?"

I reach into my bag and pull out my phone, turning it on to see that, as I suspected, Mom has called a couple of times. Of course, Owen hasn't called once. "Because I let Lily down tonight," I confess.

"Do you want to go home now?"

"Yes."

As he drives me home, I get worried about Lily. Really,

155

what if she did something really crazy? "It's so confusing," I admit.

"What?"

"How to deal with Lily. I mean, I've read some books and gone to classes, but the things I learned seemed more like the things a parent should do."

"So you're kind of like Lily's mother?"

"That's how it feels."

"Well, that seems like a pretty heavy load for someone your age, Aster."

"Yeah. But as caught as I am in this thing, Lily's caught even more."

"Like I said, I don't really have answers, but I believe that God does."

"I just wish he'd talk a little louder," I say.

George chuckles. "Yeah, don't we all."

"It's the next street," I tell him. And then we're there. "Thanks so much for, well, everything."

"Glad to be of service. And if there's anything I can do to help out, feel free to call me." He grabs his notebook, which is next to what looks like a much-used Bible, then tears out a piece of paper and scribbles down a phone number. "I mean it. Call me if I can help. God doesn't expect us to go it alone."

"Thanks." I take the paper. "I appreciate it." After I'm out of the funky old car and going into the house, I wish I'd thought to give him my number.

The lights are on in the house, but it appears that everyone has gone to bed. It also appears to have been a difficult evening for Mom and Lily. The house is a total mess. I can tell that Lily must've had a horrible tantrum, because things are thrown all over the place.

Suddenly I'm worried. What if something horrible happened? What if Mom or Lily totally lost it and—

I race to Lily's bedroom, but she isn't there. And it is a mess, as if she threw a fit. Then I bolt to the other end of the house to find that Mom is in bed and sleeping soundly. Now I'm freaked. *Where is Lily?*

I look in the bedroom I share with Rose. No Lily. In fact, Rose hasn't come home either. Not that that's so unusual.

I go to the bathroom, but the door seems to be stuck, and then I realize Lily's body is blocking it. I lean my shoulder into the door and give it a shove until it's open enough for me to slip in. Lily doesn't even move. She's curled up in front of the door in the fetal position. I get down on my knees and peer into her pale face. My heart is pounding so hard, I can hear thumping in my ears. I get close enough to see if she's breathing, then sigh in relief. Thank God, she is just fine! Then, just to make sure she's really okay, I run my fingers through her messy hair, checking her head for any lumps or bumps. She might've fallen and knocked herself out. But she seems to be in one piece. Then she makes her familiar grunting snore, and I can tell that she's simply asleep.

Still, I can only imagine why she's barricaded herself in the bathroom like this. I notice she's clutching a screwdriver in her hand. Was she planning to use it as a weapon, or was she trying to fix something? Her face is dirty and streaked with tears. Her hands are dirty too. She has on pajama bottoms, but still the same shirt that she wore today. Then I notice that her favorite pair of Capri pants, the ones she sometimes refuses to surrender to the laundry, are in the bathtub. That means she must've wet herself, because that's where I always used to put her pants so I could rinse them out before putting them in the washer. Poor Lily. She hasn't wet herself for quite some time. She must've been really upset.

Naturally, this makes me mad at Mom. *Why can't she handle Lily?* Did she make a mess of everything tonight on purpose—just to show me? Because I know I'll be stuck cleaning everything up tomorrow. And, although Mom doesn't usually go to work on Sundays, I'll bet she plans to go in tomorrow. Just to teach me a lesson. She wants to remind me that I cannot control her—that she is Mom and I am not.

"Wake up," I say to Lily, giving her a gentle shove. But she's a hard sleeper. Especially after a stressful episode. Sometimes it seems like she's in a coma. I wet a washcloth, put a little soap on it, and wash her face, which doesn't disturb her in the least. I pry the screwdriver from her hand, then wash her hands. Still, she's not moving. So I go to her bedroom, retrieve her Little Mermaid quilt, and drape it over her.

"Sleep well, Princess Lily," I say as I turn out the light.

15

"Aster? Aster? *Aster!*" Once again I wake to Lily's face just inches from mine. "Wake up, sleepyhead."

"I'm awake," I mumble as I sit up.

"Where's Rose?"

I glance over to Rose's bed, unmade as usual. It also looks unslept in. I'm pretty sure those are the same things I tossed on it when I cleaned my side of the room yesterday. "I don't know, Lily."

"I slept in the bathtub, Aster."

"No, you slept on the floor, Lily. I saw you."

She nods. "Yeah. I slept on the floor." Then she looks at me with her pale green eyes. "Mom's mean."

"Were you naughty?"

She pauses to think. "I was *mad.*"

I almost say, "Because I went somewhere without you," but then decide that's a can of worms I don't need to open. Better to start fresh today, and Lily actually seems in pretty good spirits. "Is Mom up yet?"

"Mom's gone."

"To work?"

"I dunno."

Great. Mom has taken off without even talking to me. She must be really ticked. Well, that's her problem. And her troubles are not over yet. Although I think I'm going to have to be careful. It's unfair to make Lily suffer too much.

●　　●　　●

I'm just brushing my teeth when Lily comes rushing into the bathroom. "Someone at the door, Aster!" She says this as if it's life-and-death urgent, as if it's a criminal come to pillage and plunder.

"I'll get it," I tell her. "You brush your teeth!"

Of course she doesn't do as I say. Instead she follows me to see who's at the door. Suddenly I'm worried it might be Owen. What if he's come to say he's sorry? What will I do? Will I crumble and forgive him? But to my relief and total surprise, it's Crystal.

"I tried to call your cell, but it must be off," she says.

"What's up?" I open the door wider to let her in.

"No! No! No!" Lily screams when she sees that it's Crystal. Then she grabs my arm in a vice grip and tells Crystal to go away.

"Don't have a cow, Lily, I didn't come to babysit you." Crystal rolls her eyes. "I just came by to see if you guys need a ride to church."

"Church?" Lily says. "Yes. Let's go to church, Aster."

"With Crystal?" I give Lily a shocked expression. "I thought you didn't like her."

Lily's eyes narrow as she thinks about this. "I like Crystal with you and me, Aster. Not *only* Crystal."

I nod as if this makes sense. "So can you get cleaned up and ready in time, Lily? Because we don't want to make Crystal late."

"I came early." Crystal glances at Lily as if she's the reason. But she knows that everything takes more time with Lily. I wish I could ask Crystal to help Lily get dressed so that I can take a shower, but that would be pushing it.

●　●　●

Finally Lily and I are both ready to go. I've given her a banana and granola bar to eat for breakfast on the road, and Crystal has warned her not to make a mess in the back-seat.

"I'll clean it if she does," I say quickly. I'm actually relieved that Crystal came to get us. I want to stay on her good side. "I appreciate you picking us up for church. We couldn't have gone otherwise."

"Your mom working today?"

"Mom mean!" Lily shouts with a full mouth.

"Last night Mom and Lily had a repeat of Friday night."

"Where were you?" Crystal asks. "I mean, I know you weren't at youth group."

"Aster went with Owen!" Lily spurts out. I can tell she just remembered this. "Aster left me home with Mom. She mean too!"

"You went out with Owen again?" Crystal's brows lift. "This is getting serious."

"Don't worry, I'm pretty sure it's the last time I'll go out with him."

"Good!" Lily shouts. "Owen bad, bad, bad boy."

I can't help but laugh. Sometimes I wonder if Lily has some kind of special ESP when it comes to my life, because a lot of times she is spot-on in her own weird way.

"Was Owen a bad boy?" Crystal asks.

"Sort of . . . Later, okay?"

"Yeah, sure."

● ● ●

The first car I notice in the church parking lot is George's bomb. It looks even worse in daylight. It's kind of a burgundy color with lots of rust spots. It has several dents and one of those roofs that's vinyl or something and peeling badly. George is just getting out as Crystal parks.

"Morning, ladies," George says as we get out.

"Hey, George," I say in a friendly tone that makes Lily peer curiously at him. I use a napkin to wipe banana bits and crumbs off her face and blouse.

"Who's George?" she asks, although she's staring right at him.

"I am," George says.

"Oh." Lily nods, then steps back shyly.

"George gave me a ride home last night," I say to Crystal as the four of us walk toward the church together.

She looks confused.

"Later," I say quietly as we go inside. "Sounds like worship has already started."

We all go into the sanctuary, and an usher leads us to a nearly empty row. George sits with us, but only after I make sure that Lily is next to me and not by him. She made it clear to everyone within shouting distance that she was "not going to sit by a boy!"

For that reason Crystal is sitting next to George now, and I find myself inexplicably jealous. Like he's my guy and she better keep her hands off. Okay, I know that's ridiculous. George is just a friend.

●　●　●

After church, Lily sneaks away from me. By the time I find her, she has planted herself in front of the coffee hour table, stuffing as many Oreos into her mouth as it will hold.

"Lily," I scold. "Leave some cookies for the others." Then I take her by the hand and lead her away. Fortunately, she doesn't make a scene. Well, other than the normal thing, like smiling at people with teeth that are now muddy brown from the cookies.

"I need to get home," Crystal announces when I rejoin her and George. "It's my grandparents' golden anniversary today, and my mom is doing a thing at our house."

"That's all right," I tell her. "I'm ready to go."

"Or if you want to stick around longer," George says, "I can give you girls a ride."

Lily steps up to George, as if to examine him and see if he's worthy to drive us home. "You tall," she says suddenly.

He bends down so that he's more her height. "Now I'm not."

She actually laughs. "You funny."

"You're funny too."

"We can ride with George," she tells me with Lily-like authority.

"Great," Crystal says. "Then I'll take off."

I'm relieved to see Crystal go. That way I don't have to tell her about what happened with Owen yet. I'm not ready to hear her say, "I told you so." Lily and George and I hang around until the crowd thins out. I'm not that excited to go home since I know I'll have to clean up last night's mess. Although I'm not sure why I assume that's my responsibility. After all, I did not make that mess. Although I'm aware that if I'd stayed home, that mess probably wouldn't have happened.

"I guess we should go," I finally admit to George. "Before Lily sneaks any more cookies." She's already made it to the cookie table two more times. I worry that she has an addiction to sweets. I've tried to break her, but it's like she has an inner Cookie Monster that demands something full of sugar and carbs. I wonder if I should talk to her doctor about it. What if she's getting diabetes?

"Are you worried about something?" George asks as we walk through the parking lot.

I shrug. "Not really. Just the same old, same old."

"Here we are," George says. He opens the passenger door and one of the back doors of his car.

Lily stands there staring at the vehicle like it's a three-headed dragon. "That George's car?" she asks.

"Yes. And it runs just fine. I rode in it last night."

"I not going in that," she announces, crossing her arms across her chest to show she means it.

"Fine," I say. "I am." I get in the front seat.

Aster! I hear the warning in her voice and know this can go either way.

"Do you want to walk home, Lily?"

"Yeah!"

"By yourself?"

"No! You walk too, Aster."

"No. My feet don't want to walk."

"What wrong with your feet?"

"They're tired. They stayed up too late last night."

Lily is still standing there, giving me her stubborn look.

"Do you like books, Lily?" George asks suddenly.

"Yeah." She looks suspiciously at him.

"I have a really great book that you can look at if you get in the car."

"What book?"

"I'll get it." Then he opens the trunk and returns with what looks like a manga book. He holds it up for her to see. "It has lots of pictures."

"Let me see." She reaches for the paperback, but he pulls it back, then tosses it into the backseat.

"There you go."

And just like that Lily gets in, he closes the door, and we are on our way. I thank George for his quick thinking, and he repays me by inquiring about Owen. "Did he call and apologize or anything?"

"No," I say quietly. The truth is I haven't turned my phone on since last night. But I don't want to do it now. I'm not sure how I'd react if Owen had called. Anyway, it's something I'd rather deal with in private.

"Well, if you ask me—and I know you didn't, but I'll tell you anyway—even though I never met him, I think Owen is a fool."

"Owen is a fool!" Lily parrots from the backseat.

I ignore her. "You don't go to our high school, do you, George?" I'm thinking if George goes to Jackson High, he probably would know who Owen is.

"No, I went to Davis, but I already graduated."

"Last year?"

"Actually, it was the year before."

"Aren't you kind of old for youth group?" Now I'm wondering what I'm doing with this old dude. He could be nearly twenty.

"Pastor Geoff invited me to stick around."

"Why?"

"Well, for one thing, I'm not that old. I'll be eighteen in August."

"But you've been out of high school for a year?"

"I graduated early."

"Oh." So he's an academic. I should've guessed. "Did you do college this year?"

"Yeah."

"Where?"

"Branford."

Okay, George is either smart or rich. And I'm leaning toward smart. "Do you like it?"

"Yeah. It's a great school."

"The guidance counselor at my school invited me to hear a representative from Branford next week."

"Cool. Are you going?"

"No."

"No? Why not?"

"Because there's no way I can afford a school like that."

"Then why would your guidance counselor send you an invite?"

"Who knows? I think she's just trying to be nice."

"Branford has some fantastic scholarship packages. I'm on a partial scholarship."

"Because you're a brainiac?"

"Brainiac? I haven't heard that one." He automatically turns down the street to my house. I guess he was paying attention last night.

"But is that how you got a scholarship?"

"That and soccer and because my mom went there."

"You got a soccer scholarship?"

"I wanna play soccer," Lily yells from the backseat.

"No, we're not playing soccer, Lily," I say.

"Why?"

"Because we're going home."

"But I wanna play soccer."

George chuckles as he turns into our driveway. "You got your work cut out for you, Aster."

"Tell me something I don't know." I get out of the car now and practically have to drag Lily from the backseat. She's going on about how she wants to play soccer.

"Do you want to come in the house with me?" I let go of her hand. "Or would you rather spend the day with George?" I wink at him.

But Lily actually seems to consider this, and now I'm worried she might pick George. Then what do I do?

"I'll go with you," she tells me with reluctance.

"Good." I stand up and thank George for the ride.

"Anytime."

"Lily." I nudge her. "You can tell George thank you too."

"Thanks!" She gives him a big grin, revealing once again the Oreo-stained teeth. "I like your car."

"You do?" George looks surprised.

"Yeah."

"Well, maybe I can give you a ride again sometime."

"Yeah, and we can play soccer!"

He laughs, and I just shake my head. That's Lily for you. I wave back at George as Lily and I go into the house. Neither Mom nor Rose appear to be around. And suddenly I feel concerned for Rose. What if something happened to her and nobody even noticed?

I call her cell and am relieved when she answers. "Where are you?" I demand.

"At work."

"But where were you last night?" I ask quietly so that Lily won't hear.

"Where do you think?"

"Did you spend the whole night with Jared?" I whisper.

"Duh."

"Rose!"

"Don't judge me, Aster. Jared and I are in love. We're thinking about getting a place together."

"What?"

"Oh, never mind." She sounds exasperated now. "I have to get back to work."

"Whatever."

"Don't tell Mom, Aster."

"Mom's not even speaking to me."

We say good-bye and hang up. I cannot believe that Rose is considering living with Jared. Okay, on one hand that means I get a room to myself. But on the other hand, it seems so totally stupid. What good can possibly come of it?

"Aster?" Lily calls from the family room. "I'm hungry."

"In a minute." My cell phone says I have one message. I punch the button to listen and am surprised to hear Owen's voice.

"Hey, Aster. I wanted to apologize for last night. I didn't even know you left Katie's house until pretty late, and by then I was . . . well, you know. Anyway, I'm really sorry. I'll give you a call later today."

Now I don't know whether to be happy or sad. I mean, I was so broken up over him. And then I was kind of relieved. And now I'm thinking that if a romance of a few days can be so devastatingly painful, what would it be like to be more involved? I just don't know if I can handle it. And yet . . .

16

Sunday afternoon is turning into Sunday evening, and I still haven't heard back from Owen. Why did he say he'd call if he doesn't intend to? It feels like such a setup. And now with each passing minute that he doesn't call, all I can think is that I really, really want him to call. How lame is that?

Mom came home from work around four but went to her room with a migraine, although I sort of doubt that it's for real. More likely she's trying to avoid me . . . and Lily. Of course, she didn't even ask about Rose. She probably has no idea that Rose spent the night with Jared last night. Or maybe she doesn't care. Whatever the case, I am feeling seriously frustrated with my mother.

It also occurs to me that my declaration of independence isn't going too well. How can it when Mom insists on holing up in her room? What she needs is a little more one-on-one with Lily.

That's when I decide to take George up on his offer. Didn't he say to call him if I needed help? Well, I need help!

I go into the bathroom to call so that Lily can't hear.

"What's up?" he asks.

"I want to get out of the house so that Mom can get another dose of what it's like having Lily to herself."

"Want me to come get you?"

"Would you?"

"Glad to be of assistance."

"Thanks!"

"I'll be there in about fifteen minutes."

"I'll meet you in the driveway."

So I time it, and just a couple minutes before he should be here, while Lily is still glued to a cartoon, I go to Mom's room and knock on the door. She's sitting in her recliner watching her little TV. So much for the migraine.

"I'm going out," I say quickly. "I'll be home around ten."

"But, Aster—"

"Have fun!" Then before she can get out of her recliner, I make a beeline to the door and slip out without Lily even noticing. And there, just turning down my street, is the ugly-mobile. I wave, run out to the sidewalk, and jump in. Without even turning in our driveway, George keeps going.

"Sweet," I tell him. "That was perfect."

"What do you want to do?"

"I have no idea." I dig my cell phone out of my bag and turn it off. I may turn it on later. Or not. I'm not sure. I am a little worried about Lily. But maybe Mom will get smarter in dealing with her, and things won't be quite so dramatic tonight.

George drives us around town until we stumble onto a

free concert at River Park. Apparently it's in celebration of summer solstice, the longest day of the year. I'm guessing it might feel like the longest day to my mother too. Anyway, I hope so.

I actually have a really fun time at the concert with George. We even dance in the area that's lit up with colorful lanterns. And while I'm standing in line for the restroom, George buys me this pretty wreath of flowers and ribbons to wear in my hair. I realize this isn't a date, but by the time he's taking me home, with the windows down, it is feeling rather magical . . . and almost romantic. And to my surprise, I haven't thought about Owen once!

"I hope things aren't too crazy in there," George tells me when he drops me off. I've already told him all about finding Lily in the bathroom with the screwdriver last night. "Kind of like finding Colonel Mustard in the conservatory with the lead pipe?" he asked, which made me laugh.

"At least no one was murdered," I told him.

But as I go into the house, I feel worried again. On one hand, I feel like I need to get Mom's attention. But on the other hand, I would never forgive myself if something happened to Lily.

"Go to bed!" my mom is yelling from the kitchen. "And I mean now!"

"No! No! No!" Lily screams.

I peek down the hallway to see Lily sitting stubbornly on the floor. Once again her face is streaked with tears.

"Aster!" she screams, then comes running to me as if I'm her savior. She nearly knocks me over with her bear hug.

"So you decided to come home after all?" Mom's voice sounds like it's wound tight with irritation.

"I told you I'd be home around ten."

"Well, maybe you can get Lily to bed now."

I turn and look at Mom. "Why can't you do it?"

Mom gives me the weirdest look. It's like half fury and half hopelessness. "Because you are the one who has trained her, Aster. You seem to have all the magic answers when it comes to Lily. And unless you let some of the rest of us in on your secrets, you will be the only one who can deal with her." Mom comes closer and peers into my face. "Is that what you want?"

"No, of course not. Don't you know why I've been taking off lately?"

Mom throws her hands in the air. "Because you are trying to drive me crazy?"

"Crazy, crazy, crazy!" Lily yells.

Now I realize it's time to turn this down a bit. Otherwise there will be no getting Lily to bed. "I want to talk to you later," I say to Mom. She doesn't answer, just turns and walks away.

"Come on, Princess Lily," I say in my most soothing voice.

"What's in your hair, Aster?"

"Do you like it?"

"Yeah!"

"Well, if you do a really good job getting ready for bed, I will let you wear it to sleep in, okay?"

"Is it a crown?"

"Yes." I follow her to the bathroom, where she immediately begins to peel off her clothes, and I run the water for her bath. "It's a fairy princess crown."

"Fairy princess?" Her eyes are wide.

"That's right." I pour in some bath gel and check the temperature. As she gets in, I tell her about going to the park and the music and the lanterns and even dancing with George. It's like she's enchanted, and I wonder if I really do have the magic touch. But if I do, it will be more a curse than a gift if I'm stuck taking care of Lily for all our lives.

"Why you not take me to the park?" she suddenly demands, and I realize that I may have painted myself into a corner.

"Well . . ." I consider my answer. "It's because you're not old enough yet. You'll have to wait until next year, Lily."

"I can go next year?"

"Yes," I promise. "You can."

"And can I wear the fairy princess crown?"

"Yes."

Finally she is tucked into bed, and I can't help but feel proud of my work. I almost wish Mom would pop in and see just how easy this is if you do it right, but I'm pretty sure it would only make her mad.

I listen as Lily says her prayers, and after her hearty "Amen!" I place the wreath on her head. "I now crown you Princess Lily, ruler of the fairies."

She grins and fingers a lavender ribbon. "Where *are* the fairies?"

"In your dreams," I tell her. "Maybe you'll find them if you go to sleep."

She leans back and closes her eyes. By the time I adjust the lights and get her door how she likes it, I think she's fallen asleep.

To my surprise, Mom is lurking in the hallway. "Did you get your baby to bed?" she asks.

I frown at her. "Lily isn't a baby," I say quietly.

"But you treat her like one."

I consider this as I walk to the family room. Mom follows behind me, and I get the sense that she wants to talk. Okay, that's something.

I sit down on the sofa and sigh. "Sometimes it's the only way to get her to do what I want."

"So . . . you're manipulating her?"

I stare up at my mom. "Isn't that what you do to me?"

Her brows shoot up. "What do you mean?"

"I mean, for as long as I can remember, you've manipulated me to take care of Lily—*for you*."

"I haven't manipulated you. You did it because you wanted to." She sinks into the chair across from me and leans forward with her elbows on her knees. She looks a lot older than usual. She's wearing some old faded blue sweats, and her brown hair, which is showing gray at the roots, is sticking out in odd directions. She's obviously had a rough night. Still, I am not backing down. This is a much-overdue conversation.

"You say things like, 'Only you can handle her, Aster' or 'You have the magic touch, Aster' or 'Lily responds only to you, Aster.' If that's not manipulation, what is?"

"Well, you *are* good with her. I only say those things as compliments."

"Good with her?" I frown. "Didn't you just say I treat her like a baby? That did not sound like a compliment."

"I'm tired, Aster. I'm sorry if I offended you."

"No, that's not it," I persist. "What I'm trying to say is that you've taken advantage of me, Mom. You've given me almost sole responsibility of Lily, and I never questioned it. I think I thought it was simply my lot in life. But now I'm questioning that."

She doesn't say anything.

"I mean, why is Lily my responsibility? Why am I the one who always has to take care of her?"

"I pay you to—"

"You pay me an *allowance* of forty bucks a week, Mom. Seriously, do you know how much time a caregiver would give you for that paltry sum? Maybe a couple of hours. I have Lily practically 24-7!"

"You know money is tight."

"I know that you're taking advantage of me. I know that up until very recently I have not had a life."

Her forehead creases, and I can tell she's taking this in.

"And you've probably figured out that it's no coincidence that I left Lily in your care for two days in a row."

She shrugs. "I had a feeling . . ."

"Well, I wanted you to get a nice little taste of what my life is like."

"But Lily is good with you."

"Sometimes she's good. Especially after someone like you has rocked her world so hard that when she sees me coming, it's like I'm her savior."

"But that's *your* doing, Aster. You make yourself her savior."

I bite my lip as I consider this. "I don't mean to."

"It's as if you and Lily do this dance," Mom says, "as if you know the steps, you have the rhythm down . . . and I don't know how to do it."

"It's a dance you learn by doing, Mom."

"I don't think I can learn." She shakes her head. "The last two evenings have made me feel like a total failure, Aster."

"Well, I'll admit that wasn't the best way to handle Lily. But I could help you."

"You don't understand. I work hard all day, I come home exhausted . . . I don't have the energy to deal with Lily too."

"So what does that mean?"

She shrugs, but there's a look in her eye that's hard to read.

"What, Mom? Are you thinking of putting Lily someplace? Some kind of institution?"

178

"I'm thinking it might be best for everyone."

"No!" I say. "No! No!" And then I realize I sound just like Lily now. "You can't do that, Mom. It would kill her. She needs to be with us."

"But how?" Mom's eyes are wet with tears. "You're sitting there telling me you can't care for her anymore—"

"No, I'm not saying that. I'm saying I can't keep caring for her 24-7. I'm saying I need a break. I need a life. You're the one who seems to feel unable to care for her at all. And, Mom, she is your daughter."

Tears are sliding down Mom's cheeks now, and I know I should be kinder, but it's like I can't help it. It's like all this stuff has been bottled up for too long. "I'm going to be seventeen next week, Mom. But I hadn't even had my first date until last week. I don't even have a best friend. My life revolves around Lily. And you might think she's good when she's with me, but trust me, she pulls some nasty tricks on me too. Just when I think things are going smoothly, Lily can rip the floor right out from under me."

She nods and wipes her nose on an old tissue that she's fished from a pocket. "I know . . . I know . . ."

"But here's the thing. I am not her mother. But I think in her heart she thinks that I am. I'll graduate next year. I plan to go to college." I don't mention how I'll pay tuition. "And if you don't figure out how to deal with Lily before I go—"

"I'm willing to learn," she says quietly. I can't help but think I've beaten her down. "I'm just not sure it's possible."

179

"Well, I'll admit that I might be doing some things wrong. You could be right, maybe I am treating her like a baby. Even Kellie says I do too much for Lily."

Mom nods. "You do."

"But sometimes it's just easier. I mean, do you know how hard it is to get her ready for school sometimes? And I still have to get myself ready. Some mornings I feel like I've been to war and back before I even sit down in my first class."

"I'm sorry." She looks truly sorry too. "But you do so well in school, Aster. Your grades are excellent, and you take those hard precollege classes."

"You know why I can do all that?"

"Because you're smart?"

I kind of laugh. "Smart? Or maybe I'm dumb. But it's because I don't have a life, Mom. It's because I'm always stuck at home with Lily. Naturally, I have time for homework."

"But you are smart, Aster."

"I don't know . . ."

"And you're right to confront me on this." Mom sniffs and sits up straighter. "To be honest, I'm surprised you haven't said something sooner. I think I've sort of felt like I was living on borrowed time. I'm sorry."

"But things are going to change?"

She nods. "Yes. And you're right, I am Lily's mother. I need to start acting like it."

"But Lily has another parent," I say quietly.

Mom's eyes flash. "Ha! That's what you think."

Okay, I'm trying to decide here. I've made such headway with Mom tonight, do I dare tell her about visiting Dad? Do I dare not to tell her? "You know what, Mom? I think you're doing the same thing with Dad that I do with Lily."

"What?" Her anger is now tinged with curiosity.

"You let him get away with stuff."

"What do you mean?"

"I mean, I went to visit him last week." I brace myself.

Her eyes narrow. "You went to see your father?"

I nod. "And I took Lily with me."

She looks stunned now. "Why did you do that?"

"Because I needed to find out what was going on. I needed to find out why he's not paying child support."

"And?"

"And he told me about being Mr. Mom and not paying child support in exchange for not having visiting rights. It's like he has no responsibilities at all, Mom, like he's this great big overgrown baby."

Mom almost smiles but instead lets out a deep sigh, shaking her head in a hopeless way.

"Seriously. He's playing Mr. Mom and doing whatever Jana tells him to do. And he's completely let down Rose, Lily, and me, but he acts like he can't help it because he has to stay home and play with Nelson and keep his perfect little house in order. Honestly, it makes me sick. And he was actually complaining that his life is hard. I'd love to give him a couple days with Lily in exchange for Nelson. Then he'd know what hard is."

"So what do you suggest, Aster?"

Now I smile and suppress the urge to rub my hands together. "I think it's about time he got his visitation rights back. I mean, seriously, Mom, you're doing him a favor by letting him off the hook when it comes to spending time with Lily. And she needs a daddy. Really, she does. It would be good for both of them."

"And it would give you a break."

I shrug like that hadn't occurred to me.

"But it would also give Lily a break from you."

I frown.

"She needs a break from you too, Aster. It will help her to learn to do more for herself. And you can be certain your father won't cater to her like you do." Mom really seems to be considering this scenario now. "But if Lily really wants to spend time with him, she might try to do more for herself."

"And she loves Nelson. She's really pretty good with him, Mom. And she acts kind of older, like she's the big sister for a change."

Mom actually does smile now. "Aster, I think you've come up with a good solution."

"But will Dad go for it?"

"Maybe he won't have a choice."

"Meaning?"

"Meaning he's not paying child support and I'm not pressing charges. But I could if he refuses to allow Lily to visit him."

I nod. This is exactly the way I'd hoped this would go. And

I had been prepared to push for this very thing myself, but it seems I don't need to now.

"Maybe this will all work out for the best, Aster. For all of us."

"I hope so."

Then to my surprise, Mom hugs me. I can't even remember the last time she hugged me.

17

Monday evening, after I've finally gotten Lily to bed without any magic—meaning she threw a tantrum when I tried to get her to do a few things for herself—Mom comes home and tells me that she's written my dad a letter.

"A letter?"

She nods as she sets down her purse. "It seemed the best way. I really don't think I can have a civilized conversation with that man. I made a copy of the letter for my records and sent it registered mail."

"Wow."

"Yes. I want to make sure he gets it."

"So what did you say?"

"I told him that I expect him to take some parental responsibility for his daughters. I told him that if he cannot pay child support, the least he can do is to allow visitation. And if he can't do that, I may speak to an attorney."

"Good for you, Mom." I reach up to give her a high five, and she returns it.

"I also told him that you would be managing the visitations

with Lily. I hope you don't mind. But that way you can have some control over when she'll visit, and maybe you can plan things on those days for yourself."

"Cool."

"I also spoke to someone in social services about additional supervised care for Lily—at home. They're sending me some papers to fill out."

"Thanks, Mom."

"And I'm making arrangements at work to be there less." She sighs. "It won't make any difference financially since I'm on salary."

Even so, I can tell she's not thrilled about this. I'm sure being at work sounds better than wrestling Lily to bed. "I tried to get Lily to do more for herself tonight," I say. "I'm really going to work with her. I think we'll make a chart with rewards. Lily loves rewards. Kellie has suggested this before, but it sounded like a lot of work."

"Maybe at first . . . but it might make life easier for everyone down the line." Mom smiles at me. "Let me know what I can do to help. Do you want me to look for some rewards?"

"Sure, that'd be great. I can easily make a chart on my computer."

"Good." Mom starts going through the mail. "Rose isn't home from work yet?"

"No . . ."

Mom looks at me with a curious expression. "Is there something I should know, Aster?"

"About?"

"Rose."

"You might want to give her a call."

There's no way I'm telling Mom that Rose picked up some of her things this afternoon, or that she's staying at Jared's house—actually, his parents' house, but they're on vacation for two weeks. Rose said that she and Jared are apartment shopping.

Mom just nods and continues to peruse the mail.

● ● ●

By Wednesday, Mom is fully aware that Rose has moved out with Jared. I'm surprised at how she seems to take this in stride. Or maybe she's just too tired to put up any kind of protest. Lily, on the other hand, doesn't really know what's up. For the time being, I think it's for the best, since Lily has enough to deal with right now. I've been trying to show Mom what our nightly routine is supposed to be and how Lily's chart works. But Lily has no tolerance for change and sometimes treats Mom like an intruder. She's making it especially difficult tonight, and I can tell that Mom is tired. But I have to give it to our mother, she's hanging in there. Then, just as Lily is getting out of the tub, my cell phone rings. To my surprise, Mom tells me to go ahead and take it.

I hurry to my room—my own room—and discover that it's Owen on the other end. I'm not sure how to react. I've been kind of relieved that he hasn't called. And yet I feel my heart racing just to hear his voice. Why is that?

"Hey, Aster," he says. "How's it going?"

"Okay."

"I've missed you."

"Oh . . ."

"You're not still mad at me, are you?"

"Now, remind me . . . why was I mad at you?" Okay, I know I'm acting coy, but this is the first actual conversation we've had since he let me down Saturday night.

"You mean you *weren't* mad?" He sounds hopeful.

"You know, Owen, I think I was mostly hurt. You told me that we'd go if I was uncomfortable. And I trusted you. But then when I wanted to leave, you didn't keep your word."

"I'm really sorry, Aster. I was having a nice little chat with Miles the birthday boy, and the next thing I knew you were standing there saying we had to leave."

Suddenly I feel like I'm the one who should be apologizing. But I don't.

"Anyway, are you going to give me another chance?"

"I don't know . . ." And the truth is, I *don't* know. I mean, I've been actually thinking about George lately, even wishing he'd call. And yet I know that if I placed George and Owen side by side, Owen is the one who would probably make my heart go thumpity-thump. Still, George is a great guy. Why am I so confused?

"I realize I was a jerk at the party," Owen admits. "And I shouldn't have been drinking either. The truth is, I had pretty much given that up. That's why I was looking for

187

someone like you, Aster. The kind of girl with substance, you know?"

"I know that I wasn't enjoying that party—the whole thing seemed pretty childish," I say.

"Exactly. That's why I like you. You're more mature than most girls. Anyway, I want to make it up to you. Won't you give me one last chance? There's a new movie playing, one that I think you'll really like. And we could do Greek again, if you want. Let me make last weekend up to you, okay?"

"When were you thinking?"

"How about tomorrow?"

There's a chance that Mom won't be working late tomorrow. Plus there's always my dad. I doubt that he's too busy on a Thursday evening. Besides, it's about time I make a follow-up call to Mom's letter. "Tomorrow works."

Owen says he'll pick me up around six, and I agree. I can hear Lily screaming in the hallway, so I say I have to go.

"What is wrong?" I demand as I go out to find Lily sitting on the floor with only her pajama bottoms on.

"Mom!" Lily shouts. "She mean, mean, mean."

"It sounds more like you're being mean, Lily."

"I not mean. I mad!"

I nod. "Well, mad or mean, you are not acting like a princess tonight."

"That's right," Mom says. "And I had a prize for a princess who got ready for bed on time."

"And it's a nice prize too," I add. Mom already showed me

some of the trinkets she picked up at Walgreens yesterday. We're going with a princess theme on Lily's performance chart. Mom and I also agreed on some basic rules that we adapted from a list Kellie printed out for me. Things like we won't let Lily divide us. We'll be consistent with rules, consequences, and treats. We won't cave when Lily throws a tantrum. We'll remain calm and mature with Lily. We'll make sure we're giving Lily enough time to do what she needs. And our goal will be her success—meaning a happier, more capable Lily. Of course, it's going to take time and a lot of hard work, but at least Mom and I are traveling down the same road together now.

"Remember, Lily," Mom warns her, "if you're not in your pajamas and in bed by nine, there will be no story."

Lily balls her fists and pouts.

"And no prize either," I add.

Then Mom and I go into the kitchen to wait and see if she complies. At this point I think we have about a fifty-fifty chance.

"That was Owen," I tell Mom. "He asked me out tomorrow."

Mom frowns. "I have to work late tomorrow. We're getting ready for a big sale."

"That's okay," I say. "I think it's time to call Dad."

Mom nods. "Good idea."

"The only problem will be how to get Lily over there."

"I suppose you could use my car."

We work out a plan for me to ride my bike to O'Leary's, pick up Mom's car, take Lily to Dad's, then return the car and ride my bike home. Okay, it's a lot of work, but it also buys me free time. Glorious free time.

"Why don't you call your dad while I check on Lily?" Mom suggests. "I'll be curious to hear what he has to say about all this."

So I go back into my room and dial Dad's number. Unfortunately, it's Jana who politely answers, and when she discovers it's me, her voice gets frosty. After what seems an inordinately long time, Dad comes on. "Hello, Aster." His voice is stiff and formal.

"Hey, Dad." I try to sound casual. "How's it going?"

"Well, I was just putting Nelson down."

"Seems kind of late for someone his age."

"He had a long nap this afternoon."

"Oh . . . Anyway, did you get Mom's letter?"

"Yes."

"So, does that seem fair to you?"

There's a long pause. "Fair?"

Now I realize it might be smarter not to say too much. "You know . . . I mean, all things considered . . ."

"I, uh . . . yeah, I suppose . . ."

"So, Lily would like to come visit you tomorrow."

"Tomorrow?"

"Yes. You're not busy, are you?"

"No, but—"

"And you know how much she loves Nelson. I actually think it's going to be good for her to spend time with her baby brother, Dad. It gives her the chance to be the big sister for a change."

"She was good with him, wasn't she?" I can hear a trace of optimism now. "And he liked her too."

"So, there you go. Seems like a great setup."

"And you'll be coming too, Aster?"

"Well, for a while. But then I have something else to do."

"Oh . . ."

"I better go, Dad. I'll see you tomorrow."

I hang up and hurry off to find that Lily is making it into bed in time to get a full page of her special princess stickers. She looks very pleased with herself, but Mom looks haggard.

"Guess what, Lily?" I say cheerfully.

"What?" she says without looking up from the Cinderella sticker that she's pressing onto her hand.

"We get to go visit Dad and Nelson again tomorrow."

She looks up now. "And play in the sandbox and read books?"

"Yeah. Cool, huh?"

She nods. "Cool."

Then we both listen to her prayers, and I show Mom how she likes the lights and her door. "Good night, Princess Lily," I call out, and Mom echoes.

"Good night, Princess Aster," Lily says. "Good night, Princess Mom."

This makes Mom giggle as we go down the hallway to the kitchen. "I guess that wasn't too bad," she says. We sit down across from each other at the breakfast bar.

"See," I say, "it does get easier." Then I tell her about my conversation with Dad. "He didn't sound totally pleased, but he sounded open." I don't mention that he sounded disappointed that I wasn't staying the whole time. I wonder if he thought he was acquiring a built-in babysitter. *Think again, Dad.*

● ● ●

The next morning, I get Lily to the rec center, then pick up Mom's car and drive it home. In the afternoon, I pick Lily up an hour earlier than usual, allowing me enough time to get her to Dad's, return Mom's car, and be ready to go out. Lily looks totally surprised to see that I'm driving Mom's car, but she's also pleased that we're not walking since it's hot out. As I drive, I remind her of our plans to visit Dad and Nelson, and she's even more pleased. Then, just a few blocks from Dad's house, I cautiously explain to her that I won't stay there the whole time.

"So you'll have to be really helpful," I tell her. "And take good care of Nelson and be a good big sister to him."

"I'm a good big sister." She announces this new concept with pride.

"You are."

● ● ●

Nelson is just getting up from his nap when we get there, and Dad looks as if we woke him up as well. Tough life. Lily goes directly to helping Nelson put on his saltwater sandals so they can go outside, and I visit briefly with Dad.

"Well, it looks like everything is under control," I say. "And Lily knows that I'm leaving. I think I'll spare her the big good-bye and just go."

Dad nods but looks worried. "If you think so . . ."

"I think Lily is ready for this," I assure him. "But if anything comes up, you know Mom's number. My phone might be off later."

He doesn't look too pleased about this. But I just wave and head out the door. This is his problem now. But hopefully, for Lily's sake, it'll go well.

● ● ●

I'm just pulling my bike into the garage when my cell phone rings. I am certain that it's Dad calling to tell me there's a problem and to come get Lily. But to my surprise and relief, it's Rose.

"What's up?" she asks.

I give her the quick lowdown about Lily being at Dad's house. "I'm just crossing my fingers that it'll be okay."

"Why shouldn't it? He's her father. He should help take care of her."

Of course, I could list a dozen reasons why it shouldn't be okay, but I don't. Besides, Rose sounds irritated, like something might be wrong. I mean, besides the fact that she chose to move in with Jared, which I believe is morally wrong. Not that I'm going to say as much. Well, not unless she asks. "So, how are you doing, anyway?"

"All right."

But the tone of her voice doesn't sound all right. It sounds tight and edgy and like she could be on the verge of tears. "Are you still glad you moved out?"

Now there's a pause, and I'm thinking something is not right.

"Is there a problem, Rose? Is something wrong with you and Jared? Are you sorry you moved out?"

"I don't know . . ."

I go inside the house with every possible scenario racing through my head. Jared is treating her badly. She lost her job. She is pregnant. Or maybe she realizes what a fool she's been and is sorry. "Rose, what's wrong?"

"I don't know . . . I'm just confused, I guess."

Is this her way of asking me for advice? Will I be sorry if I express an opinion here?

"Here's the thing," I begin cautiously. "I really didn't think it was a good idea for you to do this. I mean, you and Jared haven't been going together that long, and living together, well, you know how I feel about *that*. But even besides that, Rose, I know how you'd always dreamed of getting married and having the big wedding and everything, and now—"

"I wasn't calling for a lecture, Aster."

"I know. I'm just saying . . . I mean, if it was a mistake moving out . . . well, you can always come back and—"

"No way," she snaps. "I'm not saying it was a mistake. I was just feeling a little down is all. I wondered how my family was doing. Is that a crime?"

"Of course not. I just was worried about you, Rose. I thought maybe you—"

"Look, Aster, it seems to me you have enough to worry about. Between Lily and Mom, and now Dad too, your plate is full, sister. And if you ask me, you are way too codependent."

I didn't even know that Rose knew what *codependent* means. Maybe she doesn't. "What are you insinuating?" I ask.

"I'm not *insinuating* anything. I'm saying that you spend way too much time taking care of everyone else. It's like that's your life, Aster. It's like you need them to need you. And *that's* codependent."

I blink as I push the key into the lock. So she does know what the word means. And something about what she's saying has a ring of truth to it. The kind of truth that stings a little. And yet she's not totally on track here.

"Well," I say sharply as I go into the house, "you don't know everything about me, Rose."

"Really." She sounds unconvinced. I can just imagine her examining a perfect fingernail, a bored expression on her face. So I tell her about my big date tonight. In fact, I probably make it sound much bigger than it really is. Or maybe I'm just being optimistic.

195

"Hey, maybe there's hope for you yet," Rose says.

"I'm doing the best I can," I say as I drop my bag on the counter. "But it's not like I can just abandon everyone." *Not like you did*, I want to add, but don't.

"No, I don't expect you could."

Okay, now I don't know what to say. Apparently she doesn't either. There's a long silence, and then she sighs loudly. "Well, I better go. Tell Mom I called, okay?"

"Want me to tell Lily hi for you too?"

"Yeah . . . whatever."

"Take care."

We both hang up, and I decide that I'm not going to let Rose get to me tonight. Sure, I can tell she's unhappy about something—probably just her stupid decision to move in with Jared. Talk about jumping out of the frying pan and into the fire. Anyway, I just hope that she doesn't do something really insane like getting pregnant. Honestly, I was afraid that was what she was going to tell me.

But I am not going to think about that now. Here I am with only me and my own life to focus on for a pleasant change. Why not enjoy it? Besides, didn't Rose just lecture me about being codependent? Why shouldn't I take her advice and think about myself instead of her?

I cannot even describe how absolutely fantastic it feels to be *home alone*. Or to be in my *own* room, a room I share with no one, although I suppose that could change at any given moment if things with Jared and Rose don't go smoothly. Plus a lot of Rose's junk is still in here, although I might box it up in a week or so and put it in the garage.

As I get ready for my date, I still can't believe I've pulled this off—this brand-new sort of freedom. To be able to take a shower and fix my hair without having to sneak around, without having Lily asking me what I'm doing and why, without having to make sure everything is all set for her.

I turn on my CD player, loud, and I actually dance for a while, daydreaming about that night when Owen and I danced in the parking lot at the Greek restaurant. I take all the time I want to primp. I even use a pale pink shade of Rose's fingernail polish to do my fingernails and then my toenails.

As I do these things, I also pray that all is well with Lily and Dad. I need things to be well with Lily and Dad. This could be the beginning of my whole new life!

18

It's weird, but tonight's date is starting to feel like a rerun of the last time we ate at the Greek restaurant. Only not as much fun. I'm not even sure why that is, but I suspect it has to do with what happened at Katie's house on Saturday night. It's sort of like I've put my guard up against Owen. Like I'm not really sure I can trust him anymore. Like some of that old magic is gone. And, sadly, there is no dancing in the parking lot after dinner.

"Miles and Katie are meeting us at the movie," Owen says as he drives across town.

"Oh . . ." Now, for some reason I don't receive this as good news. And I feel sort of tricked by it. I mean, why didn't he tell me sooner?

"Is that okay?"

"Yeah, sure," I say. And, really, why isn't it okay? But there's just something . . . something about this whole evening that bugs me.

We get to the theater, and Miles and Katie have already gone through the line and purchased our tickets with theirs.

Owen pays Miles back, and Katie announces that she needs to powder her nose. I actually need a potty break myself, so the guys give us our tickets and say they'll get seats and meet us inside the theater.

After using the toilet, Katie and I stand in front of the poorly lit mirror, and I touch up my lip gloss while Katie actually does powder her nose. Go figure.

"It's so cool that you're not holding Saturday night against Owen," she says. She snaps her compact closed and drops it into what looks like a really expensive designer bag. Katie has always had a taste for the "finer" things.

"He told you about *that*?"

She kind of shrugs. "Well, he didn't really have to tell me anything. I mean, it was kind of obvious why you left, Aster."

"Obvious?" I actually thought I'd been rather subtle. I don't recall anyone seeing me slipping out. They were too wasted to notice.

"And, seriously, who could blame you for taking off?" She gives me a quirky smile.

Okay, I am truly puzzled. "You mean because of the drinking, right?"

Now Katie looks puzzled. "Huh? The drinking?"

"The reason I left."

"No, I mean because of Emily Davenport."

"What?"

Katie's hand flies up to her mouth. "Uh-oh . . ." Now she turns to leave the restroom, but I hold on to her arm.

"What are you saying, Katie?"

"Nothing."

"Come on," I urge her with a forced smile. "You can tell me. We're old friends. What about Emily Davenport?" I don't know much about Emily, except that she's very pretty and has this obnoxious laugh that sounds like a chicken cackling.

"Well, Emily pretty much threw herself at Owen that night, Aster. Everyone saw it. Anyway, you shouldn't hold it against him."

"Hold what against him?"

"Oh, you know."

I want to shout at her in a Lily-like way, saying that I don't know and she better tell me! But instead, I act all chill and calm, like no big deal. "Oh, you mean they slept together."

Her eyes grow wide as she nods. "But really, Owen was pretty much wasted by then. I don't think he really meant to . . ."

"No, of course not."

"So, you're not mad, are you?"

"No," I say calmly. "I'm not."

And the truth is, I'm not mad. Not really. In a way I'm actually feeling somewhat relieved. Okay, I suppose I'm a little hurt too. Or maybe it's just my pride that's taken a blow. But I don't feel angry. And yet I have no desire to sit next to Owen now. I know I can't pretend like I still care about him. And I cannot sit through an entire movie like everything is just peachy keen. I think by then I really would be mad.

Just as we get back to the lobby, my cell phone starts ringing. "I better get this," I tell Katie. Actually, I'm relieved for this little break. That is, until I see that it's my dad's number, which cannot be good.

"Hello?"

"Aster," Dad says in a quiet voice. "There's, uh, there's been an accident."

"*What?*"

"It's Lily. She fell and maybe broke her arm."

"What? What happened? How did she—"

"Can you come?"

"Come? Where?"

"The hospital. Lily is asking for you. She needs you."

"I don't have a car, Dad." Then I realize that the hospital is only a few blocks away from the theater. "But that's okay. I can be there in a few minutes. Tell Lily I'm on my way." I snap my phone shut, then hurry to where Katie is waiting. "I have to go," I tell her. "My sister is in the hospital, and—"

"Is it serious? Do you need a ride? Should we get the—"

I quickly explain it's a broken arm, but that Lily is very upset. "You know how she can get?"

Katie nods with serious eyes. "Oh yeah."

"Anyway, I'll just run over there. Tell Owen what's up, okay?"

"Yeah, sure."

I turn and hurry out of the theater with my ticket still in hand. I see an older woman at the end of the line, so I shove the ticket toward her. "Here," I say. "Pass it forward." Then I start running down the street toward the hospital. Poor Lily!

I have some very mixed emotions as I run. On one hand, I feel like I just made a good escape from Owen and an uncomfortable situation. On the other hand, I'm really worried about Lily. She hates hospitals, and any kind of medical treatment totally freaks her.

As I turn toward the hospital entrance, I start to feel angry at Owen. How dare he ask me out, acting like nothing was wrong, after he'd slept with Emily Davenport at a party that he'd taken *me* to! But then I think about Lily and wonder how she broke her arm. Wasn't Dad watching her? What kind of parent is he, anyway?

Finally I'm there at the ER, and Dad is in the waiting area. Just Dad by himself. No Jana or Nelson, which is actually a relief. "Where is Lily?"

"Through that door," he says. "She's making a lot of noise in there. I'm sure you'll find her easily enough."

He's right. She is making a lot of noise, screaming "No, no, no!" over and over. And I do find her, huddled in the corner of the examining room. "Lily," I say in my most comforting voice.

"Aster!" she screams with wild eyes, running toward me.

I go to her and put my arms around her. "It's okay," I say soothingly. "Everything is okay."

"I need to give her a shot," the nurse informs me. "Can you get her to the examining table?"

Lily's eyes are full of fear. "No shot! No shot! No shot!"

"Shh, shh," I say, eyeing the nurse as if to hint that this is not a good moment and can't she just wait. "Calm down, Princess Lily," I say as I ease her over to the table. "Just sit down, okay?"

"You sit down too," she says.

And so I do. "You hurt your arm," I tell her, "but it's going to be okay. Everything is going to be okay. The nice nurse just wants to help you." I stroke her back and glance at the nurse, who is not looking particularly nice or kind as she approaches with a hypodermic needle all ready to shoot. Fortunately, Lily's back is to her now. But she's still sobbing and clinging to me with her good arm, which I notice is her right arm. A small relief since Lily's right-handed.

"What is that?" I quietly ask the nurse, nodding to her needle, which she is tapping and holding high.

"Sedative," she says quietly. "We need to calm her down so we can set the arm."

"Oh, okay." I nod. Of course, there's no way Lily will let them touch her arm without being sedated.

I rub Lily's back and talk quietly to her as the nurse aims the needle for Lily's upper right arm. Then in one swift movement that I cannot help but admire, she shoves the needle into the pale flesh, shoots it in, and pulls it out. Of course, Lily lets out a loud yelp. But that's the end of it.

"Nicely done," I say quietly.

"Thanks for helping." The nurse offers me a smile.

It's not long before the sedative takes effect, and the nurse and doctor are helping a much calmer Lily to lie down on the table. I hold her good hand and stroke her sweaty hair while the doctor and nurse work together to set her broken arm. To everyone's relief, she lets out only a couple of little puppylike whimpers. And then she closes her eyes and falls asleep.

"What now?" I ask the nurse.

"We'll put her in a cast, and when she wakes up in an hour or so, she can probably go home."

I nod. "Okay. I'm going to go talk to my dad."

The nurse looks slightly worried, like she's afraid she'll be stuck holding a tiger by the tail again. "But you will come back, won't you?"

I suppress a laugh. "Yes. In a few minutes."

"Good."

Dad looks understandably stressed when I find him in the waiting area. I can't even imagine what he's been through simply getting Lily here tonight. "How is she?" he asks with what seems genuine concern.

I give him the lowdown, and then there's a thick silence between us. I wonder if he's blaming me for all this. Maybe it is my fault. If I hadn't been so selfish, wanting my freedom and all, maybe none of this would've happened. And why did I sacrifice Lily—or her arm—like this? For a stupid date with a stupid boy who is so not worth it! I feel like kicking something.

"I suppose you want to know what happened," Dad says.

I turn and study Dad. He's running his fingers through his beard with a faraway look in his eyes. I suspect he wishes he were somewhere else. With someone else. I sigh as I imagine Lily pulling one of her horrible tantrums this evening. Some nasty fit that probably resulted in some stupid stunt that broke her arm and created havoc in our father's otherwise rather calm and peaceful life. Still, we might as well get it over with.

"Yeah," I finally say, "what happened?"

"Lily and Nelson had actually been getting along really well," he begins slowly. "In fact, I was rather enjoying having Lily there. It gave me a little break with Nelson. Being an only child, he can be kind of demanding. He expects me to play and entertain him all day long. It gets old."

I nod and suppress the urge to say, "Tell me about it." My dad's been through enough for one day.

"So anyway, we'd made it through dinner without too much fuss and mess. And Lily was actually trying to help Nelson get ready for bed." He chuckles. "Which was rather amusing. She definitely has her own way of doing things."

"Kind of like the blind leading the blind."

He nods. "I was up there sort of supervising them when I heard Jana come home from her shift. She usually gets there shortly before Nelson's bedtime, just in time to say good night. Anyway, I hadn't told her about the whole visitation thing or Lily coming. I know I should've. But I also knew she wouldn't be too keen on the idea."

"So she didn't even know Lily was there?"

"No. And I thought I should probably tip her off so she wouldn't say something, you know, in front of Lily."

"Right."

"But Jana was already upstairs, and I was about to explain what was going on when Nelson came streaking by in nothing but his Sesame Street shorts. And Lily was running behind him, yelling something. I'm sure they were just playing some kind of silly game, but Jana thought Lily was trying to hurt him."

"Lily would never hurt—"

"I know. But Jana reacted anyway. I guess it was like that mother bear instinct."

I feel my eyes growing wider now. "What happened?"

"Jana gave Lily a little shove, you know, to keep her away from Nelson, and Lily tripped over this stupid rug that Jana insists we need at the top of the stairs, and, well, she fell . . . down the stairs."

"Lily fell down the stairs?" I'm trying to wrap my head around this scene, to picture it in my mind. But all I can imagine is an enraged Jana shoving poor Lily down the stairs, which I'm sure isn't right. But that's what I'm seeing.

He nods. "Fortunately, Lily didn't fall all the way down the stairs, the landing midway stopped her. But I heard the snap on the second step."

"Poor Lily."

"Yeah. I'm really sorry about this, Aster."

"Is Jana sorry too?"

Dad gets a funny look now. "Well, of course," he says quickly.

Still, that's all the answer I need. Jana probably isn't sorry. She probably thinks she was simply protecting her son. Whatever.

"Anyway, I had to give a report to the social worker here."

"In case there was abuse involved?" I ask with what I'm sure is a suspicious look.

"Well, because she's a juvenile, and it's an injury . . ."

"And you told them the same thing you told me?"

"Not exactly. I mean, not word for word."

"Did you tell them about Jana's involvement, Dad? Did you tell them that Jana pushed Lily?"

He looks down at his lap.

"You didn't, did you?"

He glances around like he's nervous, then he lowers his voice. "How can I, Aster? She works here. In this very hospital. How would it sound?"

"Like the truth."

"You don't understand."

I shrug. "I think I do, Dad. Anyway, I need to go be with Lily. That sedative will wear off, and she might get scared again."

He nods.

●　●　●

As I sit with Lily, I am feeling furious with my dad. I feel like this is his fault. Like if he'd been doing what he should be doing as a dad, none of this would've happened. Okay, I know

207

that's unfair. But it's how I feel. Then suddenly I realize that I forgot to ask him if he'd called Mom. I'd wager he hasn't.

I call home and tell Mom the whole story. Well, not the whole story. I tell her that Lily is here, her nice pink cast is on, and she'll be waking up soon.

"Oh, dear. Should I come and get you girls?"

I consider this. On one hand, it doesn't seem too much to expect our own father, the man who is somewhat responsible for Lily's broken arm, to drive us home. On the other hand, I'm so mad at him and his stupid wife right now, I'm not sure I can keep my words in check.

"No," I finally say. "Dad's already here. He might as well bring us home."

"Okay."

• • •

Lily is still a little dopey when they wheel her out to Dad's car, but at least she's in fairly good spirits. And she seems happy to see Dad.

"Where's Nelson?" she asks.

"In bed by now," Dad says as he buckles her into the backseat. He's actually being really careful with her. "How are you feeling, Lily?"

"I feel good," she tells him. "I like my cast."

"It sure is pink," I say.

"Pretty pink."

I sit in front with Dad. And I'm beginning to feel guilty for having such hard feelings toward him. Really, this isn't his fault. Although I do think Jana should take some of the blame. Then I realize, no, she's letting him take it for her. In fact, Dad is pretty much caught in the middle here. Kind of like I am. Or was. I'm still determined to get out of my trap. Dad, on the other hand, may be stuck in his trap for some time.

"I'm sorry about your arm," Dad tells Lily as we both help her into the house. Her legs are still a little wobbly from the sedative. But if we can get her safely in, she should sleep well tonight. "I hope it gets better soon."

"So I can play with Nelson."

There's a long pause. Then Dad says, "Yes. Nelson would like that."

Of course, Dad and I both know that Jana might not feel the same way. But that's Dad's problem at the moment.

Finally we have Lily settled in her bed, and Dad says good night and leaves. Then Mom comes in and asks Lily how she's doing.

"I fell down," Lily mutters sleepily.

"I know." Mom leans down and kisses her forehead. "I'm sorry about your arm, Lily."

"That's okay." Lily's expression is serious. "It's pink."

Then Mom leaves, and I finish tucking Lily in. Finally I say, "Good night, Princess Lily with the pretty pink cast." Lily smiles and closes her eyes. She's still in her clothes, but there is no way I'll force her into pajamas or teethbrushing tonight. We both deserve a break.

19

I find Mom in the family room. She is pacing back and forth with a deep crease between her brows.

"Are you okay?"

She stops and nods, then sits down on the sofa. "Just thinking."

"About?"

"Oh, you know . . . everything. Lily, you, Rose, your dad. It seems like everything is a mess, Aster. And I can't help but think it's partly my fault."

I consider this and think, *Yeah, it has to be partly your fault.* Of course, I don't say this. I mean, Mom has made great strides lately. Why should I kick her when she's down?

"The thing is, I've blamed your dad, Aster. For years I have blamed him for everything."

"Well, he did leave you, Mom. You can certainly blame him for that. Right?"

She doesn't answer.

"I mean, it was his choice to go, you didn't force him," I say.

"And then this whole deal of not paying child support. You can blame him for that too."

"I was thinking even farther back, Aster."

"What?"

"Well, the truth is, I've been angry at your dad ever since Lily was born." She looks directly at me now. "There. I've said it."

"Why?"

"I blamed him for Lily's condition."

"You blamed him?" Now, this doesn't compute. How could Dad be responsible? Her condition is not even a genetic thing, not that you can blame anyone for the DNA they toss to an unborn child.

"I went into labor around midnight, but he didn't want to take me to the hospital too soon."

I nod.

"We didn't have good insurance. And with both you and Rose, I'd had long labors, and those hours add up. So your dad thought we should wait until my water broke."

"Don't lots of people do that?"

"Yes. But even so, I had a bad feeling about not going in, and I told him so."

"But he still didn't want to go?"

"He said it'd be better to wait. Then we could have Mrs. Stein from next door come over and stay with you girls. Otherwise, we'd have to wake you up and take you."

"I remember Mrs. Stein. She was nice."

Mom nods, but I can tell her mind is still on that night. "So we stayed home, and I kept having contractions. At about six my water broke, your dad called Mrs. Stein, and we headed for the hospital. Of course, by the time we got there and I was in the delivery room and hooked up to the monitor, almost an hour had gone by. Something was wrong, but the baby's head was already crowning, and the doctor wanted her out fast. He did a forceps delivery, and when Lily came out she was blue."

Now I recall what I read about the flattened umbilical cord and no oxygen getting to the baby. "So if you'd gone to the hospital sooner . . . Lily might've been okay?"

"Yes, that's what I believed. And so I blamed your father for Lily's brain damage."

"Oh . . ."

"I never told anyone about this before, Aster. I mean, about blaming him. I didn't even tell your father . . . well, not in so many words. But he knew. I hinted at it. And I was angry. And I know I made him miserable. But I was miserable. Life was miserable."

I go over and sit next to my mom on the sofa. I put an arm around her shoulders. And I realize that I'm crying. I don't know what to say. Maybe words don't matter. Then she hugs me, and we both cry a little, then pull away, suddenly uncomfortable with all this emotion and closeness.

I go into the kitchen and get us both tissues, then sit back down. "You know, Mom, I was blaming Dad for Lily's arm tonight. I was thinking, 'Crud, Dad, I take care of Lily for her whole life and she never breaks a single bone, and you have her for a few hours and the next thing we know she's in the hospital. Nice work.'"

Mom sort of smiles at this.

"But then as we were coming home, I realized that I need to forgive him."

Mom sighs. "Maybe so . . . but how is that possible?"

"In my case, it's going to take some help from God," I admit. "But he's the one who says we need to forgive. So I'm thinking he ought to be able to help me with it."

She just nods.

"And I'm sure if you asked him, Mom, he'd help you too."

"I'll be keeping that in mind, Aster. Let me know how it goes for you, okay?" Then she gets up and yawns. "Now I'm heading for bed." She pauses. "Oh yeah, the guidance counselor from your school called me at work today."

"Ms. Grieves called you at work?" I'm astounded. "Why?"

Mom smiles. "She said you're very smart. And I told her I was aware of that."

"She called just to tell you I'm smart?"

"No, she called to ask me to encourage you to take these scholarship opportunities seriously, Aster. She says you have an excellent chance for something really good."

"What does that mean?"

"It means that she wants you to come to that meeting to-morrow."

"Huh?"

"For Branford University."

"Oh yeah. I remember."

"I told her that I'd heard Branford was pretty expensive. And then she told me something, Aster. Something you never mentioned."

"What?"

"Your SAT scores."

I just shrug.

"She said you received the highest in the school."

Okay, this is news to me. "Seriously?"

"And not just for this year, Aster. She said the highest ever."

Now I'm stunned. "Why didn't anyone tell me this?"

Mom laughs. "I guess they assumed that you were so smart you must know it."

I just shake my head. "I had no idea."

"Well, do us all a favor and go to that meeting tomorrow. It seems that the recruiters from Branford are seriously scouting you."

"What about Lily? She won't be going to the rec center tomorrow, will she?"

Mom frowns now. "Well, Lily is my responsibility. I'll think of something."

Suddenly I remember George and his offer to help me. He said to just call. "I have a friend," I tell Mom. "And Lily actually likes him."

"Him?"

"He's a nice Christian guy and very responsible. He's actually helping Pastor Geoff with youth group."

Mom considers this. "I don't know about a guy. Do you really trust him, Aster?"

I nod firmly. "I do. And the meeting will probably be only an hour or two. In fact, maybe George could drop me off and take Lily to the library."

"Perfect!" Mom seems sold.

Perfect, I'm thinking, but only if George is available and willing. If not, well, maybe it's just God's way of saying that some expensive private college isn't what I need.

Still, as I get ready for bed I think about my SAT scores. I had no idea they were that high. Oh, I knew they were good. But the highest in the school—ever? That's pretty mind-blowing.

After I'm in bed, I ask God to help me forgive my dad. But even as I say this, I realize that I already have. I also realize that God's been helping me with a lot of things all along. And so I thank him. From the bottom of my heart, I thank him.

20

"I can't think of anything I'd rather do than drop you off at a recruitment meeting for Branford," George says after I call him the next morning. "I think you'd really like it there. Not that I'm biased or anything."

"And Lily? You don't mind taking her to the library?"

"Not at all. I happen to have a great fondness for libraries."

Then I explain about her arm. "But she's feeling lots better today. And she's very proud of her pretty pink cast."

"We'll go show it off."

Shortly after I call George, my phone rings, and when I see that it's Owen, I'm tempted to let it go to voicemail. Then I think I should just get this over with. Besides, I'm glad to know the truth about him. Despite my wounded pride, I feel I have dodged a bullet.

"How's Lily?" he asks after we've said hello.

I give him a quick lowdown.

"That's good to hear." He pauses. "So how about you and

me, Aster? Are we still good? Katie was acting a little weird last night. Like maybe you told her something about us?"

"No, not really. I just had to leave for Lily's sake."

"Oh, good."

"And I sort of need to get going."

"What's up?"

I tell him about the recruitment meeting.

"Branford?" He chuckles. "Are you serious? Do you know how much their tuition is, Aster?"

"Not specifically."

"Well, that's where Wayne went last year." He laughs even louder. "Trust me, their tuition is pretty steep. My dad is still complaining about it."

"Oh." I'm so tempted to tell Owen about my SAT scores and that Branford is actually scouting me. But I think, *Why bother?*

"Seriously, Aster, you'd just be wasting your time."

"Well, it's my time to waste."

"Hey, if you have time to waste, why not waste it with me? We could drive out to the lake and—"

"No thanks."

"Maybe later then?"

"I'm going to cut to the chase, Owen. I'm just not interested, okay?"

"Not interested in what?"

"In dating you."

There's a long silence.

"Sorry to be so blunt," I say. "But I thought you should know."

"And now that you mention it, Aster, I was going to tell you that this whole thing with your retarded sister . . . well, that's just not going to work for me."

"Yeah, I'm not that surprised."

And then, without even saying good-bye, I hear a loud click. Owen hung up on me. Why does that not surprise me?

And why hadn't I paid more attention to the signals earlier on? And why hadn't I believed what Crystal told me? Probably because I didn't want to. Owen represented independence to me—and yet being with Owen turned into a different kind of bondage.

● ● ●

Lily's cast makes getting her ready even more of a challenge, but I try to stick to the plan that Mom and I have agreed on. I encourage her to do as much for herself as possible. And when she complains, I point out that she is getting to do a very grown-up thing today. "You are going to the library with George while I go to a meeting at my school. It's going to be just you and George, Lily. And I expect you to act very grown-up."

"Is it a date?" she asks with wide eyes.

"Sort of like a date," I tell her. I figure this can't hurt since Lily doesn't really know what a date is.

"Cool." She smiles at her reflection in the mirror as she

makes a good attempt to get the brush through her hair with her good hand.

Soon we're in George's car, and I'm a little worried that Lily might freak over seeing me dropped off without her, but to my amazed relief she simply waves and smiles. Very grown-up.

The meeting goes better than I could've imagined. Naturally, the recruiter can't make any promises, but she gives me all the paperwork and encourages me to follow through on everything.

"I hear you play soccer too," she says as we're leaving.

"I do, but it's not like I'm a star."

"Well, we have a solid women's team, but they're always looking for new players—not stars." She winks. "And you'll have to come visit us next fall. I put the brochure about that weekend in your packet."

"I have a friend who goes to Branford," I say as we leave the meeting room.

"What's her name?"

"It's a guy. George . . . George . . . you know, I can't remember his last name." The truth is, I don't even know his last name. "But he's from New Zealand, and he's a really nice guy."

"That has to be George McBride. And you're right, he is a really nice guy."

When I get outside the school, I see that old burgundy car parked in front. And Lily is sitting in the passenger side of the front seat, waving out the window with her good arm and grinning like a cat that just ate a canary.

I jog over and see that George is grinning too. "Sorry, Aster, but you've been demoted to the backseat."

"That's fine," I say as I climb in. Then I throw back my head and start laughing. I laugh so hard that I practically have tears coming.

"What? What?" Lily demands. "What is funny? You laughing at me, *Aster*?"

"No, not at all." I wipe my eyes and catch my breath. "I'm just laughing because I'm so happy, Lily. And you know what?"

"What?"

"I just realized that today is my birthday! I am seventeen!"

"Happy birthday, Aster!" Lily shouts.

"Happy birthday," George adds. "That makes me think we should go out and celebrate. Anyone here want some cake and ice cream?"

"I do! I do!" Lily shouts.

"Me too!" I shout back. "I scream, you scream, we all scream for ice cream."

"Stop! Stop!" Lily yells. "Stop the car!"

Without questioning her, George puts on his signal and pulls over. "What's wrong, Lily?" he asks calmly.

"Aster!" she yells. "It really your birthday?"

"Yes," I answer. "I just told you that." Suddenly I remember how jealous Lily can be about my birthday. It comes a couple weeks before hers, and she always thinks it's unfair that it's not her birthday too. In fact, I often share my birthday with her.

"Get outta car!" Lily yells.

"Why?" I ask.

"It your birthday—you sit in front."

"Oh, that's okay, Lily."

"No, Aster! It your birthday. You sit in front!" Now she's trying to undo her seat belt with one hand. "Come on, *Aster!*"

"I'm coming. I'm coming." So I hop out, open her door, and help her to unbuckle and get out of the car. Then I notice that George's old car has a bench seat in front. "Hey, there's room for three," I tell Lily. "We can all sit in front."

"We all sit in front!" Lily says.

So I slide in, and Lily slides in next to me. I close the door and buckle her back in, then turn to look at George. "Is this okay?"

His face breaks into a big grin. "Absolutely."

"I scream, I scream," Lily cries. "I scream for ice cream!"

"That was close," I tell her. Then I repeat the silly rhyme the right way so she can try again. And as George pulls back into traffic and Lily chants about ice cream, I realize that once again I am stuck in the middle. But this time I'm liking it.

I lean back into the seat, listening as my sister and George break into a very off-key rendition of "Happy Birthday," and I realize that my life really is good. Oh, it might not always go smoothly. Okay, it hardly ever goes smoothly. And it'll probably never resemble anything close to normal. But it's my life—and I thank God that he is in the middle of it.

Melody Carlson is the award-winning author of around two hundred books, many of them for teens, including the Diary of a Teenage Girl series, the TrueColors series, and the Carter House Girls series. She and her husband met years ago while volunteering as Young Life counselors. They continue to serve on the Young Life adult committee in central Oregon today. Visit Melody's website at www.melodycarlson.com.

START STUDYING THE BIBLE FOR ALL IT'S WORTH!

Maybe you've heard this before: "Jesus is the Rock." But what does it really mean? And what does it mean to you personally? Find out in these devotionals on the words of Jesus from bestselling author Melody Carlson.

 Revell
a division of Baker Publishing Group
www.RevellBooks.com

Available wherever books are sold